T0044133

WHEN AMONG CROWS

WHEN AMONG CROWS

VERONICA ROTH

TOR

TOR PUBLISHING GROUP

NEW YORK

WHEN AMONG CROWS

Copyright © 2024 by Veronica Roth

A Tor Book
Published by Tom Doherty Associates / Tor Publishing Group
120 Broadway
New York, NY 10271

www.torpublishinggroup.com

Tor® is a registered trademark of Macmillan Publishing Group, LLC.

The Library of Congress Cataloging-in-Publication Data is available upon request.

ISBN 978-1-250-85548-0 (hardcover)
ISBN 978-1-250-85549-7 (ebook)

Our books may be purchased in bulk for promotional, educational, or business use. Please contact your local bookseller or the Macmillan Corporate and Premium Sales Department at 1-800-221-7945, extension 5442, or by email at MacmillanSpecialMarkets@macmillan.com.

First Edition: 2024

Printed in the United States of America

0 9 8 7 6 5 4 3 2 1

For the Rydzes,
who love words as much as I do

Kiedy wejdziesz między wrony musisz krakać tak jak one.*

—Polish saying

*When among crows, you must caw as one.

WHEN
AMONG
CROWS

A PRELUDE

This isn't the forest guardian's usual haunt. Every other day of the year, he stands guard over the huddle of trees in the Montrose Point Bird Sanctuary along Lake Michigan, where the water's stink is rich as chocolate to his bone-dry nose. But every year in June, on Kupala Night, he makes the journey to St. Stanislaus Kostka Church in West Town to guard the fern flower as it blooms.

He doesn't like it here. He doesn't like how his hooves sound on the wood floor, sharp and echoing. He doesn't like the ceiling that blocks his view of the stars. And he doesn't like religious spaces, in general—the obsession with wrong and right, purity and pollution, modernity and eternity, it doesn't make sense to him.

But this is a natural place for deep magic, because it was bought at a great price. People came from the old country to the new to earn their bread, and they scraped the very bottoms of their wallets to build this place for themselves, though their wallets were not very deep. That kind of sacrifice creates a debt, and there's nothing magic likes better than the great hollow of a debt. And so magic nestled here, heedless of what the adherents of this particular religion would think of it. It draws the leszy here, too.

The sanctuary is still and silent. The leszy tilts his horned head back to look at the mural painted on the dome above him. All the host of heaven, perched on clouds, stare back down at him.

The sanctuary doors open, and when the leszy lowers his head, a mortal man stands at the end of the aisle.

Unearthly smoke curls around the man's black boots, the remnants of a sacred fire. There are many sacred fires lit on Kupala Night; this man must have leapt across one, to receive its blessing. Likewise, there's a spray of white flowers—wormwood—tucked into one of his buttonholes, no doubt plucked from a vila's crown of greenery. If the leszy's senses hadn't already told him this man wasn't ordinary, those two blessings would have done so. He came prepared for the task at hand.

And there is only one task that could possibly be at hand: plucking the fern flower when it blooms.

The man stops at a distance from the leszy, and holds his hands behind his back like a soldier at ease. He looks wary, but not frightened, and that's stranger than all the rest of him.

He only comes up to the leszy's breastbone, and he's half as broad. The leszy has the body of a man stretched beyond its capacity—long arms that end in big, clawed hands; sturdy, split hooves; and a stag's skull as a head. His staff is the size of a sapling. Moss grows on his broad, flat shoulders, and flowers bloom in his eye sockets.

"Turn back," the leszy says. His voice is like a tree tilting in the wind.

"My lord leszy," the mortal man says to him, with a quick bow. "There are rumors of the fern flower in Edgebrook Woods and in all the parks that border Lake Michigan."

"Then what reason can he possibly have for coming here?" the leszy asks.

The man tilts his head. His hair is the gray-brown color as the tree bark in the leszy's usual sanctuary. His eyes are the same shade, as if painted with the same brush.

"One thing all the rumors have in common is you," the man says. "So I followed you here."

The leszy stands in silence. He remembers very little about his journey from the Montrose Point Bird Sanctuary earlier that day. Cacophonous streets crowded with metal and plastic. Air thickened by exhaust. The sky crowded by buildings. He was guided only by his own sense of purpose—*A holy kind of purpose,* he thinks, with the mural of the heavenly host still staring down at him.

He doesn't recall the man. But since the man stands before him with no apparent motive for deception, the leszy supposes he's to be believed.

"So where does it bloom? In the courtyard? In the stoup of holy water?" The man tilts his head again, and a mischievous smile curls his lip. "In the altar?"

There's something in the cadence of his voice that the leszy recognizes from long ago.

The leszy came here as so many of his kind did, less

than a century ago, to escape the cruelty of the Holy Order that hunts all creatures who walk or crawl this earth. They came among mortals who were escaping other cruelties—mortal ones, though no less harrowing for it. He thinks fondly of the refuge those mortals offered him, the kinship they found in shared pain and shared escape.

He dwelt elsewhere before, playing guardian to a small patch of woods in the old country, right along a river, as is his preference. But he came here to escort a mortal woman. Or more accurately—to escort the plant that the woman carried. A fern swollen with the potential to flower on Kupala Night.

She, too, was driven by almost-holy purpose, unable to explain her attachment to the plant that she carried across the sea. He can feel the dirt that she scraped from beneath her fingernails after she lifted the fern from its pot to place it upon the altar, and the roots of the plant twisting into the stone there, impossibly. He can smell the incense from the thurible and he can hear, somehow, the chanting voice of Baba Jaga, the one who bewitched them all—

"What is he?" the leszy asks the man.

"I am a supplicant," the man replies.

"He is a fool. Turn back."

"I know you guard the fern flower. I know you're tasked with keeping out the unworthy. How do I prove to you that I'm worthy?"

"He expects answers but does not give them. Turn back."

"I am," the man says gently, "a supplicant. And I won't turn back."

The leszy leans into his staff. The man has now refused him three times.

"A contest," the leszy says. "If he wins it, I will stand aside. If he loses it, he will turn back."

"A contest of what?"

"Something he can do that I can also do. Does he dance?"

The man smiles. "No, my lord. Not unless enchanted by vila." He taps a toe on the floor, to draw attention to the trace of sacred fire still clinging to his boots.

"Does he sing?"

The man shakes his head.

"He is raised to violence, as all of his kind are," the leszy says. "Perhaps he can wield a bow."

"As it happens," the man says. "Yes."

The leszy nods. He raises his staff—an old branch, crooked and dry—and suffuses it with life to make it pliant, like a young sapling. Then he reaches up to his eye socket, and plucks one of the flowers that grows there. It comes out with blossom and stem and white root all together, pinched between his claws.

All the plants of his forest owe him a debt, so when the leszy asks, the plant responds, growing long and thick as string. He fastens each end of it to the now-bent staff to make a bow.

The man watches. He marvels, as a mortal marvels, but his breath doesn't catch.

The leszy has known men for centuries. The ones who know how to see him also know that they should fear him.

The only ones who don't fear him are the ones who prefer him dead. This one is an oddity, neither fearful nor murderous.

"What is he?" the leszy asks again, picking up a pencil from the nearest pew to grow it longer and sharper, so it resembles an arrow.

"I'm a supplicant," the man says. "That's all."

"It's not 'all,' or even much of anything."

"It's enough."

The leszy can't argue with that. Having finished fashioning the bow and two arrows, he sets them aside on a pew while he finds a target. Though he doesn't share this mortal reverence for the saints, he doesn't like the idea of using one of them as target practice. It seems unwise.

The leszy urges one of the plants in his eye socket to bloom, filling the space of the one he plucked. He points at one of the paintings on the wall diagonal from him. They're fixed between the windows, each one depicting a significant moment: a man on a cross, a man multiplying bread and fish, a woman washing a man's feet. But this one is in a garden.

"The target will be that one's eye," the leszy says.

At the mortal man's raised eyebrow, the leszy adds, "Surely you do not object to the eye of a snake as a target?"

"My objection is to the defacing of private property. I have no interest in getting arrested," the man admits.

"I will mend it when we are finished."

The man nods. The leszy nocks the arrow and draws the bow taut. He breathes the musty smell of incense. He releases the arrow, and it stabs directly into the eye of the serpent, curled around a young woman's ankle in the Garden of Eden.

He then offers the bow to the man.

"If he nestles his arrow beside mine," the leszy says, "I will consider him the victor."

The man takes the bow from him. At first, the leszy isn't sure he'll have the strength to draw it—the leszy is much larger than the man, and if he were ordinary, he wouldn't even be able to pull the string. But whatever he is, he's stronger than most. He places the arrow and draws it, and breathes deep and slow.

Even before he releases the arrow, the leszy knows the man won't win. His hands are too unsteady on the bow, the weapon too big for him. The arrow buries itself in the serpent's throat, just below the target. The man's head drops, and he offers the bow back to the leszy.

It's only then that his hands tremble.

"Please," the man says.

The leszy has heard men say a thousand things. Dares and challenges, questions and demands, prayers and bargains. He has rarely heard them beg.

"Please," the man repeats. "I know enchantments surround the fern flower, and they'll test me. All I ask is that you let me be tested."

The leszy detaches the string from the bow, and straightens it, dries it, stiffens it until it becomes his staff again.

"Many have sought the fern flower," the leszy says. "They seek a talisman that will bring them happiness and wealth, power and wisdom. Or they wish to trade it so they can carve a new path for themselves, or bring illumination to their short and dark lives. Sometimes, the most selfless among them even seek special healing for brothers and sisters, mothers and fathers, friends and lovers. For which of these purposes does he seek the fern flower?"

"None," the man replies. "I seek it for a stranger. A . . . creature."

The leszy knows that men lie. He tilts his head back to look at the ceiling again, the crowd of people draped in robes and listening to holy pronouncements.

"Kupala Night is a night of whims," the leszy says, and he steps aside, gesturing to the altar behind him.

"Thank you," the man says softly.

"Once he faces this test, he may wish he hadn't thanked me."

With a tap of his staff, the enchantment that shrouds the altar lifts. Growing from the center of the stone top is a lush green fern.

The flower is about to bloom. The air feels like a stitch drawn taut against a hem, or lips braced against a whistle. The man walks past the leszy to the altar, and it's fitting, the leszy supposes, that someone who calls himself a supplicant should approach an altar in this way.

Something shifts in the center of the fern: a stem. It grows like a drawbridge raising, the leaves around it creaking and shuffling to accommodate it. It grows like time speeding forward, but only in this sliver of space that the fern occupies. The leszy watches as the bud of the flower swells, and when it breaks open, the man falls to his knees. He reaches for the flower, but halfheartedly, as if he doesn't expect to touch it.

And indeed he doesn't.

Power surges in the air. It rages around the man like a powerful wind, though the pages of the hymnals left open on the benches and the delicate violets in the leszy's eye sockets don't stir with its force. It's so strong that it lifts the man from the ground and splays his limbs, as if he's a puppet raised by its strings.

The man screams, but only for a moment before the force—whatever it is—wraps around his mouth and silences him. His fingers constrict in the air at odd angles, as if they're breaking—no, they're the spasms of someone in pain.

The leszy steps back down the aisle when the girl appears.

She's young. Hardly more than a child. Small, with sallow cheeks and a bare rib cage instead of a chest, though the rest of her appears to be covered in flesh. Beating in the rib cage is a heart, black as tar, that follows the same syncopated rhythm as a human heart. Her eyes are milky white all the way through. She carries a sickle far larger than she is, with a wicked, gleaming blade.

She is a południca—a noonwraith. She's not at home in the dark any more than the leszy is at home indoors. But for the fern flower, she makes an exception. All of those whom Baba Jaga tasks with its protection do.

She looks up at the man, and blinks slowly.

"What is within you?" Her voice is high and girlish. She tilts her head to the other side, the movement a little too fast, a little too bent. "I must know."

She drums her fingers on her breastbone, and the man collapses to the ground, the force holding him up disappearing. She bends down and wraps her long, clawed fingers around his jaw. She wrenches his face toward hers. He's trembling, and his eyes are full of tears.

"Give me your name, and I will be able to open your heart," she says.

His next breath shudders on the exhale, and he doesn't respond. He is watching her black heart pulsing between the rib-bars of its cage.

"I must open your heart to determine if you are worthy of this prize," she says.

His tongue darts out to wet his lips. He says, in a weak, cracking voice: "Dymitr."

"Dymitr," she whispers, and she releases him.

She steps back and sits on the edge of the altar, and the leaves of the fern stretch toward her. She wears a ragged white dress, tattered at the hem and open across her bone torso. She drums her sternum again, considering the man. Then she gestures, sudden and sharp.

The man gasps, and his shirt opens over the chest, baring the red rosette he painted over his heart—another protective symbol, the leszy notes—

And then a spray of blood strikes the altar like a dusting of holy water as his skin peels away from his chest—

And then muscle and bone, cracking and breaking apart, though his screams are, yet again, inaudible—

And the leszy stares at the man's heart, pulsing red and strong in his chest. Blood trickles down the man's breast-bone. The noonwraith's eyes glow like the moon. She taps a claw against her lips.

"Oh, my," she says softly, after a moment. It's a sigh, and the leszy can't tell what kind.

"What is it you see, my lady?" the leszy finally dares to ask.

She looks at him as if only just noticing him, though they've met before. Few mortals make it to this point, but "few" is not "none."

"He will have the flower," the noonwraith says.

"My lady?"

"That is my word. And my word is my word."

With that, she turns and walks away, and with each step she takes into the church sanctuary, she descends far-ther into the earth, as if walking down a staircase. The man's ribs knit together over his heart, and his muscle and skin layer back over bone, and he collapses forward with a moan. He is sweat-soaked and trembling.

And just out of reach in front of him: the soft red light of the fern flower, now in full bloom.

2

A LATE SHOWING

His grandmother was the one who taught him how to spot them. She took him to the town center and sat him down at Basia's Cafe for a coffee and a biscuit, right by the window so they could look out at the street. He was only twelve years old, so a coffee with foamed milk with the woman who liked to wink conspiratorially at him across the dinner table was a rare treat.

"Look across the way there," she said, pointing a crooked finger out the window. "At the bank, at the market—someone there is not right. Can you tell me who it is?"

He'd been tested before, but only verbally. *What does a strzyga turn into when provoked?* "An owl—well, a creature the size of a human, with an owl's face, an owl's wings—and *claws*—" *When does a wraith appear?* "Any time of day, unless it's a noonwraith, and then it thrives in sunlight." But this . . . *Can you tell me who it is?* How was he supposed to know?

Dymitr sipped the thick foam dusted with cinnamon that covered his coffee, and searched for the face that wasn't like other faces in the little crowd across the street. At the bank, a man in a wide-brimmed hat stopped at the

ATM to get cash. As he turned to tuck it into his wallet, Dymitr saw him in profile. Nothing unusual in the dusting of whiskers and the watery blue eyes.

A little girl stopped to pick up something on the side of the road. As she crouched with flat heels, her red skirt brushed the damp bricks, and her mother tapped her on the head to get her to stand. She did, lifting what looked like a hoop earring to the light. Nothing unusual about her face, either.

Just behind them was a woman alone, middle-aged, with brown hair tied at the base of her neck. She raised an apple to her nose, one of the yellow ones with shiny red patches. Ordinary.

"I could guess," he said. "But it would be random."

His grandmother smiled. "I told your father you were wise."

The woman set the apple down and picked up another one. This one she hardly looked at before tucking it into her shopping bag.

"Watch me carefully," his grandmother said, and he set down his mug. She breathed deep, and her hand tightened. She dug into her palm with her fingernails, and then—he saw a red glint in her eyes, brief as a bolt of lightning.

"It's her," she said, her voice rougher than before. She pointed to the woman with the apple.

"What did you do?" he asked.

"When you become one of us, you will tap into a wellspring of power within yourself," she said to him. "You can unleash the full extent of that power, or you can let in only a trickle of it—and when you do so, you will see the monstrous parts of our world for what they really are. It requires tremendous control, but you are capable of it. You will *become* capable of it."

Dymitr nodded, though he couldn't imagine what she meant.

"What is she?" he asked, nodding to the woman across the way. He had reached the bottom of the foam in his cup, and the first bitter taste of coffee touched his lips as he drank.

"She is a zmora," Grandmother said. "Have you studied them yet?"

"Zmora," he said. "A nightmare?"

"In a manner of speaking." Grandmother snorted a little. She scratched at the age spot that kissed her cheekbone. "The old stories say they wear the faces of women and creep into a man's bedroom to perch on his chest, pour horrors into his mind, and drink down his life force. He wakes exhausted, not knowing why." She shrugged. "Like all of the old stories, there is a little truth and a lot of fancy."

"What do they eat, then?" He'd learned that was always the most important question.

"Fear," she replied.

He watched the woman approach the register. If the cashier sensed there was something strange about her, he didn't let on. He peered into her shopping bag and started to tally what was inside it.

"The old stories also say they're shapeshifters, and can turn into a crow, or a horse, or a stoat—or even a hair, slight enough to slip through a keyhole." Grandmother shook her head. "Nonsense. But they can make you see whatever they want."

Her hand trembled ever so slightly as she lifted her coffee cup to her mouth.

"Don't be fooled by her human face, her human voice," she said. "That is no woman."

🐦

The Crow Theater doesn't have a sign. Instead, a row of neon birds, each in a different stage of flight, blinks above the marquee. Today the marquee reads:

ALIENS VS. GHOSTS: WHO WOULD WIN?
Alien (1979) vs. *The Haunting* (1963)—**Double Feature**

The theater itself is a sagging, scuffed place in Edgewater, one of Chicago's northernmost neighborhoods. It shows only horror movies, though it seems to treat "horror" as an umbrella term for anything that might unsettle or disgust. Showings from the past week, as listed on the theater's threadbare website, include a vampire movie from the early aughts where everyone was in skintight patent leather, a documentary on cane toads, and *Jaws*.

A man with ash-brown hair bypasses the box office and steps into the adjoining bar, Toil and Trouble. He passes beneath a cluster of sparkly bats when he steps down into the space, his shoes sticking to the floor a little as he walks. The bar top has been designed to look like a closed coffin, and perched on top of it is a mechanical witch that cackles every time the bartender passes it.

He knows without looking at the bartender that she's not human. He's gotten good at sensing it without seeing it, that undefinable *something* that he can almost taste. But he doubts any of the other patrons have noticed.

He shrugs the soft guitar case from his shoulders and leans it against the bar, then sits down to wait. His contact sent a message to the owner of this establishment requesting a meeting, but he has no way of knowing if Klara Dryja will actually show up. He's ten minutes early, regardless.

Above him a string of lights made to look like flickering candles dangles a little too close to his head. He ducks to read the menu scribbled on the far wall in messy chalk handwriting. The zmora bartender sidles up to him.

Though there's still a chill in the air outside, she's dressed like it's the middle of summer, her arms bare, pale as milk. Her hair is cropped close to her head, but her high cheekbones and square jaw remind him of the place he just left. They should. All zmora are Polish, like he is, though they have creature cousins all over the world.

"Can I get you something?" the zmora asks. She sounds American.

It's so strange to speak to her like she's the same as him, but he's getting used to it. "Would I be a fool to order wine here?"

"It'll taste a little like feet, and it'll come in a chalice the size of a melon," she says. "Does that interest you?"

He pretends to consider this.

"I'll have a beer," he says. "Whatever you like best."

"Good choice."

There's an array of drinkware just behind the bar: a mug with cat eyes painted on it, a goblet with snakes wrapping around its base, a cup shaped like a human skull. She sets a bottle of beer down in front of him and then raises a glow-in-the-dark plastic cup at him in question. He shakes his head.

The bartender reaches for a rag, setting off the cackling witch, whose pointed hat bobs as she bounces with laughter. The bartender curses, and turns the witch to face the wall.

He's suppressing a smile at this when someone at his shoulder clears her throat.

She's a small, slight woman with the sly smile of a fox and hoop earrings the size of his fist. That she's a zmora is more obvious for her than it is for the bartender—there's too much *time* in her eyes. Klara Dryja is her name, and she's the one he's here to meet.

"You." She says it as if it's a certainty. "Come with me."

"You must be Klara," he replies.

"Must I?" She's already stepping out of the bar and into the movie theater lobby beside it.

He leaves a ten-dollar bill on the bar, picks up his guitar case and his beer, and hurries after Klara. The air smells burnt and buttery. She leads him down a short hallway plastered with old movie posters, past the restrooms and both of the theater's two screens, up a flight of stairs and into a projection room. On the screen, Sigourney Weaver stands in a spaceship wearing a white tank top and underwear.

A man just inside the projection room glances at them, then draws the curtains across the windows. He's sitting beside a stack of film reels in tin cases.

"Thank you, Tom," Klara says to him. She turns back to Dymitr with eyebrows raised.

"Who are you?" she says.

"I came to make you an offer."

Klara smiles, and her smile is a warning. "That's not an answer."

"I know better than to just *give* you my name," he replies, and he hooks his finger around the neck of the beer bottle to raise it to his lips.

She doesn't stop smiling, but the hint of amusement in her eyes disappears.

"So you know a little about magic," she says. "You know that a name is powerful. And you know, I assume, what this place is?"

He shrugs. "A nightly buffet, laid for creatures who feast on human fear? Yes. I know."

"You make us sound so uncultured." She gestures to the curtains. "Playing in that room is the movie *Alien*. 1979. Ridley Scott. A symphony of tension, rising to shock, disgust, horror. Mellowing to a tremulous kind of anxiety. For those zmory with far more delicate palates than most—for the rest, we offer a slasher movie every Wednesday. Quick, hot scares, like a plate of french fries." She touches her hand to her belly. "Delicious. But not particularly refined."

"Fascinating." He swallows more beer.

Klara cocks her head. "It doesn't alarm you at all. That you're among monsters who consider you a food source. You *are* human, aren't you?"

"I'm human," he says. "But I'm not easily frightened."

"How very annoying." She leans against the wall and tucks her hands into her pockets. "What are you, then? Oś-wiecony? Or your zmora mother bore a human boy? Or you have a zmora girlfriend? How do you know what we are?"

Oświecony. Her mouth forms the word with ease. She speaks Polish, but sounds American; someone caught in between worlds in more than one way.

"Does it matter?"

"You show up here with something to offer me, but you won't give me your name and you won't tell me how you're aware of us," she says. "Why do you expect me to listen? Or really, I should be asking . . ." She pulls away from the wall, and moves closer—too close; her proximity makes the hair on his arms stand on end. "Why do you expect me to spare your life?"

"We share a mother country. Maybe I'm counting on that to stay your hand."

"I share a mother country with a lot of people, and they don't always mean well," she says. "I've threatened you, and you're still not afraid. You must have a very good offer for me."

Dymitr smiles at her. "If you promise not to kill me, I'll give you my name in exchange."

Klara rolls her eyes. "I promise you'll leave this place alive and intact if you pose no threat to us. Good enough?"

"Sure." He sets his beer bottle down on the table next to the film reels. "My name is Dymitr."

He can't feel the weight of the name, but he thinks she can. A name is a gift, but a name is also a weapon. It makes him vulnerable to her. She can use it to find him, even to curse him. She could, in theory, give it to someone else on his behalf, but she won't. If she did, its power would be lost; no one can use it against him unless he's the one to hand it over.

She replies, "Stop wasting my time, Dymitr."

Dymitr doesn't know much about Klara Dryja. She's the youngest of the Dryja family's three leaders, and the most receptive to humans, of which each family has a handful. Not all babies born to zmory are zmory, after all. Humans born to creatures—or monsters, as some call them—are "oświecony": enlightened. Aware of the creature world, or the World That Endures, as Dymitr's mother calls it, since it's full of beings with long lifespans.

His contact told him that the other two leaders of the Dryja family won't even speak to their oświecony, and instead funnel all communication through other, lower-status zmory. So though Klara's ferocity is well-known, she's still the most likely to listen to him.

He touches a hand to the paper in his pocket.

"I heard a rumor," he says. "That one of your number is under a curse."

Klara works her jaw. She's not smiling now. "Did you."

He nods. "I heard this curse degrades its victim day by day, tormenting them with visions until they lose touch with reality."

The room goes dark around them. He stiffens as not just the walls, but the floor and ceiling disappear, leaving the two of them standing in a void. He knows that all zmory are skilled illusionists, but it's one thing to know that, and another to be caught in one of their illusions.

Klara tugs something from her hair: a long, sharp needle with a decorative spider at the end of it. She turns it in her fingers.

"I mean no harm," he says, in his gentlest voice. "I simply want you to know that I understand how much suffering this curse inflicts. And I know . . ."

He takes the paper out of his pocket. As he does, Klara raises the needle to his throat, poking the point into his skin just enough for him to feel it. He holds up the paper so she can see it. Her eyes have gone as black as the void that surrounds them.

Slowly he unfolds the paper, revealing the red flower nestled inside it. The petals emit a gentle glow.

The illusion falls away from Klara's eyes, as well as the room around them. He relaxes a little as the floor reappears beneath him.

"I know that the fern flower unravels most curses," he says. "But it can only be touched by mortal hands."

Klara's eyes stay locked on the fern flower.

"How did you get that?" she says, her voice rough.

"I was tested," he replies.

The memory of his own heart pulsing in front of him, of the bare, dry rib cage of the wraith, swells in his throat like a pill too big and too dry to swallow. He breathes, in and out, in and out, aware that he's now been quiet for far too long.

Klara sniffs, and smiles a little, presumably as she tastes his panic.

"I was tested, and I was found worthy," he goes on. "A fact you should not take lightly."

He folds the paper over the flower again, and tucks it into his pocket. Then he touches her wrist, guiding the needle away from his neck. She allows him to.

"What is it you expect in return?" she says.

"That is between me and your cursed zmora," he replies. "So if you would tell me how to find them, I would be grateful."

Klara slides the needle back into the knot of hair at the back of her head, and smooths down the front of her shirt. She glances at Tom, still sitting at the projector and playing solitaire on his phone, as if nothing is happening behind him.

"Tempting though that offer is," she says, "I can't give you what you ask for without knowing what you want. I have to protect my people."

"You are afraid of a human?"

"A normal one, no," she says. "But the Holy Order blend in too easily, and they have killed too many of us."

Dymitr looks at Tom, who has just won at solitaire, the cards spilling across his screen.

"Fine. I'll tell you," he says. "I seek an audience with Baba Jaga."

Klara looks a little surprised. He doesn't blame her; most humans aren't stupid enough to look for Baba Jaga. She's a powerful witch—*the* powerful witch. She who defeated Koschei the Deathless; she who lures children and maidens and knights alike into dark tangles of trees and sells them favors at too high a cost; who rides a mortar and pestle and lives in a house that stands on chicken legs. Fearsome, eternal, capricious Baba Jaga.

"What makes you think that the zmora you're looking for will know how to find her?"

He shrugs. "I think she'll know more than I do, which is a start. Or perhaps you'll share something useful with me on her behalf."

"And when you don't get anywhere," Klara says. "What will you do? Renege on your side of the deal?"

"I'll get somewhere."

"I know human men," she says. "I have made their worst nightmares come to life around them. I have made them weep. I know what happens when they don't get what they want from us." Her voice lowers to a whisper. "They get angry. They seek out a member of the Holy Order. And they have us killed."

The Holy Order—the bogeyman of the bogeymen. She speaks of them the way his mother used to speak of Baba Jaga stealing his toes if he didn't stop running in the hallway. He wonders what kinds of stories the zmory tell their children to scare them into behaving. Do they tell them the Holy Order split their souls to make their swords? That they have to wrench them from a sheath of vertebrae every time they fight?

He asks, "What will it take to convince you that I mean no harm?"

"There's nothing you can say or do that will convince me of that," Klara says. "Men always mean harm. The question is simply 'when'."

She gestures to the door, dismissing him.

"If you change your mind," he says, "I'll be at the Thorndale Red Line stop at midnight. I'll wait for half an hour."

He picks up his beer bottle, shoulders his guitar case, and leaves the projection room with the fern flower heavy in his pocket.

He's walking down a dark stretch of Clark Street, past a defunct furniture store with EVERYTHING MUST GO scrawled on one of the windows, when he hears the footsteps. They lack the purpose of someone walking home, and the purposelessness of someone stumbling away from a bar. They're light and even, and when he stops, they stop.

He straightens the straps of the guitar case he wears on

his back, and steps backward into the pool of light cast by a streetlamp. At the edge of the circle that lights the cracked concrete, he sees a pair of glittering eyes.

"Can we hurry this up?" he says. "I know you're following me, so you may as well reveal yourself."

He expects a zmora, maybe; someone who sniffed him out at the theater and decided to find out what he was up to. Or a wraith, some cousin to the noonwraith who flayed him open and has her own use for the fern flower in his pocket. What he isn't expecting is a woman.

Specifically his sister, Elza.

She has the same cool brown hair as him, though she wears hers in a braid, and the same mouth—too full for a man, his older brother used to say, teasing, as he poked Dymitr in the lip. But her eyes are honey-warm in color, and there's a dimple in her left cheek even when she isn't smiling.

"I don't know how you can stand to talk to them like that," she says, with an exaggerated shudder. "They want to *eat* you, you know."

He scowls at her and demands, in Polish: "What the hell are you doing here?"

"Keeping you from doing something stupid," she replies. "Father told me you had left on some fool's errand—"

"I proposed a mission based on information I collected in the field," Dymitr says, and he can hear how his voice changes when he uses official language, pitched lower and without inflection. "Grandmother approved it. So I'm sure Father didn't tell you it was a *fool's errand*—"

"No, I decided that all by myself," Elza says, scowling right back at him.

She's dressed for a fight, her black boots laced tight and her black canvas pants loose enough to allow movement. When she's not anticipating danger, Elza loves ruffles and bows, airy fabric that floats around her body like gossamer, bright lipstick and pointed shoes. Fragile, impractical things that fill her closet with color.

"Baba Jaga is your target?" she says. "Really?"

"I'm not discussing this with you."

"Funny, I thought that's what we were doing right now." She rolls her eyes. "If you're going to do this, you'll need backup—"

"Backup will get me killed," he replies. "I need to be as unobtrusive as possible, I can't charge in with the entire Order at my back—"

"I didn't realize you thought of me as an entire army unto myself." She folds her arms, and he can see a knife sheathed along her forearm, the handle peeking out from her jacket sleeve. "I'm not stupid, Dymek. I know you didn't propose a mission in *America* just because, what? You stumbled across some random tip—"

"A thread connects this place and ours, and it has for almost two hundred years," he says. "Today I ordered gołabki at a diner and didn't even have to speak a word of English."

"Yes, the wonders of Polonia never cease." She reaches for his arm, pinches the sleeve right over his elbow. "I know you. You're acting strange. Tell me why."

"I," he says, stepping toward her, "am doing what's necessary. And if Grandmother thought I needed you here, she would have sent you." He lowers his voice, hardens it. "If I wanted you here, I would have asked you."

He tugs his arm from her grasp, and steps back.

"Go home, Elza," he says, and he leaves his sister standing in the circle of light, a crease between her eyebrows.

3

A RED LINE

Every train station has magic in it, not that Ala can feel it. Some of her kind swear they can smell it, and maybe they can; all zmory have good noses, but hers is average at best.

It's because of how they were built—the train stations, that is, not the noses. They were hoisted above Chicago's brick buildings in the mid-1910s, with the city refusing to close down cross streets for their construction, so the builders had to get creative. It took them over a decade to complete just the Red Line.

There's always sacrifice in building something that's never been built before, and sacrifice creates a debt, and debts create a space for magic to rush in. So if the Thorndale Red Line stop hums with it, well—that makes sense to her.

The station is empty at this hour, with the trains running every fifteen minutes or so, depending. She pays for a single-ride pass and pushes through the barrier. As she climbs the steps to the platform, the Purple Line Express rushes past in a smear of greenish light and chattering college students on their way to Evanston.

Slumped on one of the benches under the awning is an

old woman with a battered suitcase between her feet—not who Ala is looking for. But at the end of the concrete, leaning against a pillar, is a young man, probably in his late twenties, his hair a dusty shade of brown and his hands tucked into the pockets of his jacket.

Bingo.

She recognizes him from the bar. He ordered red wine—no, beer, after she told him about the chalice she was required to serve the former in. He had an accent and a nice smile, if you're interested in that kind of thing. Ala isn't.

She's tempted to just take the fern flower from his pocket. Tom told her which one it was in—right, not left, and wrapped in paper, so she could probably get away with touching it, even though quasi-mortals aren't supposed to be able to. She could distract him with an illusion and pick his pocket, no problem. She's done it before.

And maybe she still will, she thinks. But first she has questions.

He pulls away from the pillar as she approaches. He still has that guitar case on his back, soft and definitely not shaped like a guitar is inside it.

"You're Dymitr?" she demands.

He smiles a little. "She gave you my name?"

"I asked for it. I'm not interested in cursing you," Ala says.

"And you are . . . ?"

She hesitates. But there's little danger in giving out her own name. She's already cursed, after all.

"Aleksja," she says. "But everyone calls me Ala."

There's a chill in the air here, from the wind off the lake. She's glad she borrowed Tom's zip-up for the walk, even though it smells like pipe tobacco and men's deodorant.

"So you're a bartender," he says. "Not every zmora could work in a customer service job without scaring off the customers."

His accent reminds Ala of her mother. The way she lisped a little and consonants fell heavy from her lips. It's been many years since she died, more than Ala cares to count, but she can still hear the woman's voice, exhorting her to sit up straight or to run a comb through her hair.

"Who says I don't scare them?" she says. "The Crow is a feeding ground. It's not exactly dependent on liquor sales from Toil and Trouble." She looks toward the lake, where two white apartment buildings stand right next to the water, just barely visible now in the moonlight. "I don't believe in angels, you know."

"Come again?"

"You show up out of nowhere with this remedy to my little *condition*," she says. "And it's like you expect me to think you only mean well, only . . . I don't believe in angels."

If she had to guess, she would say he looks . . . *sad*. But the expression is fleeting.

"Do you believe in a simple exchange?" he says. "I was clear about my motives. I'll give you the fern flower if you help me get to Baba Jaga. Simple as that."

Ala laughs.

"Why the hell do you want to meet with Baba Jaga?" she says. "I'm given to understand that most mortals leave her presence owing more than they received."

For the first time, he seems at a loss for words. He holds the guitar case against his stomach, pinching it in such a way that makes her think something much slimmer takes up space inside it.

"My reasons are my own," he says. "But I suspect you're desperate enough to agree even if you don't know them."

"Fuck you," Ala says automatically, but he's right, and she can't pretend that he isn't.

The curse found her a few years ago, constricting her chest like a gasp and prickling behind her eyes. At first, it showed her brief visions, easily banished. But then it crept across her days, taking up minutes, and then hours. Tormenting her.

Killing her, just as it killed her mother—by inches.

"I know what haunts you," he begins.

"You have no idea what haunts me. How could you possibly?"

He reaches for her, and she's too unused to this—a mortal who doesn't fear her, a mortal who would dare to touch her cold skin—to pull away. His fingers close around her wrist, so gently she could break his grip without even trying. Just enough to get her attention.

"Show me, then." His eyes are gray-brown, like a military jacket, like a tree trunk in winter. "Make sure I understand."

Ala needs no further invitation. She tugs her wrist free from his grasp, and makes the world fall away.

Not every zmora is equally good at illusions, just like not every zmora has an equally good nose. Ala has a talent for the former, if not the latter.

The Thorndale platform disappears: the awning, the heaters (switched off now that it's no longer winter), the old woman and her suitcase, the benches, the screens that predict the arrival of the next train, and the tall buildings near the lake.

In its place is a forest. The trees that surround them are dense, with narrow white trunks and branches that tangle together just above their heads, untrimmed and untamed. The layer of leaves beneath their feet is wet and soft, as if from a recent melting. Ala can almost smell the rot.

The sun has set, but it's still light enough to see by. A tall, hulking man with a shaved head stands between her and Dymitr, his scalp shining with sweat. He stands over a long-haired woman with a greenish cast to her skin. She kneels on the ground in a white nightgown. She's a rusalka—a water maiden.

Dirt streaks the fabric right over her knees, and blood. Blood on her sleeves, on her back. Stripes of it, soaking through the white.

Ala tries to meet Dymitr's eyes, but he's staring, rapt, at the man with the shaved head. The man reaches behind him and digs his fingers into the skin at the back of his neck. Then he yanks both hands up in one strong motion, and a bone-white blade pulls free of his flesh, his blood still running down the hilt. He may have split his soul to make the weapon, but he still has to pay for it in pain every time he wants to fight with it.

A purple-red color, like a port-wine birthmark, spills into his fingers and palms, all the way over his wrists, like he's plunged his hands in a vat of red dye. His eyes, too, glint red, bloodshot all the way through.

He's a Knight of the Holy Order, and he's here to perform an execution.

The rusalka wraps her too-long, too-thin arms around herself, and hunches over her bloodied knees, sobbing.

"Please," she says softly. "Please—"

The man's sword drips blood onto the wet leaves. He swings it. Dymitr and Ala both jerk back at the same time. As the rusalka's head rolls toward Ala, the man, the leaves, and the birch trees all disappear. The Thorndale platform takes their place just as a train pulls into the station.

Ala watches the late-night commuters step out of the cars—just two of them, a woman in blue scrubs and a man still wearing his warmest coat, unzipped over a worn sweater. The old woman with the suitcase waddles onto the train. The doors close; the commuters descend to the street; the train pulls away from the platform.

They're alone.

Dymitr's Adam's apple bobs as he swallows, hard.

"You see memories," he says roughly.

He doesn't ask who the man was, and how he managed to draw a sword from his spine as if it were a sheath. That means he must already know who the Holy Order are.

She tastes something sour. He seems friendly enough—certainly none of *them,* or anyone aligned with them, would ever speak to someone like her as if she's an equal, as he does—but maybe he's called on them before, just to rid his neighborhood of something *pesky.* It wouldn't surprise her. Humans are always talking out of both sides of their mouths.

"Maybe they're memories," she says, shrugging. "Maybe they're hallucinations. I don't know, and I don't particularly care. What matters is, they're bloody, and they fill my every waking moment. So take a moment to consider whether you're toying with me or not, because if you are, I'll kill you."

"I'm not." She's not sure a mortal has ever spoken to her that gently before.

"Well, I don't know how to find Baba Jaga, let alone how to get her to meet with some random human," she says. "So now what? You have a fern flower and no leads."

"You don't know anyone who might be able to help us?" He raises his eyebrows. "Can't get me into a place I could never otherwise go?"

Ala sighs.

As it happens, she can.

"How long will that thing live?" she says, nodding toward his right pocket.

"Thirty-six hours before it's no longer useful to us," he says. "Why?"

"I have an idea," she says. "And it's five hours until

sunrise, so we might still be able to pull it off if we get moving."

She sends a series of texts as Dymitr summons a ride with his several-generations-old iPhone. She doesn't know how he can even read anything on a screen that cracked. But there's an air of carelessness about him in general: the stretched, misshapen collar of his T-shirt, the fraying ends of his shoelaces, his rumpled hair, his bitten fingernails. As if he hasn't looked in a mirror in quite some time—or perhaps he has, and he doesn't care about what he sees.

"Why is it called the 'Crow Theater'?" Dymitr asks her. "Some Poe reference?"

Ala shakes her head. "It's from that saying. 'When among crows, you must caw as they do.' Because we're supposed to fit in among mortals. Mimic them."

"Cheeky," Dymitr says. "Considering they're the ones who compare *you* to crows. And ravens. And—"

"Stoats, yeah," Ala says. "Klara thinks it's funny."

Her phone buzzes, and she glances at the new message. *You're in. But hurry up.*

Luckily, at that moment a puttering Honda pulls up to the curb in front of Dymitr, and he ducks his head in to check that it's theirs. Ala slides in after him, and sneezes. It smells like old cigarettes, stale french fries, and a pine-scented air freshener, so potently that when she meets the driver's eyes in the rearview mirror, she can hardly smell the sugary nervousness he emits. She gives him a broad smile, the kind that tends to make mortals uneasy, and the sweet smell of his fear surges into her nose. Her mouth waters.

She glances at Dymitr, who's watching her like he knows exactly what she's doing. He rolls his eyes.

"You're going all the way to . . . uh, Ninety-Second?" the driver says, frowning at the phone fixed to his dashboard. "Didn't even know the streets went up that high."

"Well," Ala says. "You should get out more."

The driver pulls onto Lake Shore Drive, which will take them south all the way past downtown, past Hyde Park, and right up to the invisible line that divides Illinois from Indiana. On the Illinois side of the line is an old warehouse that makes containers—bottles, cans, jars, and the like—during the day. At night, though, it's something different.

"Are you going to tell me where we're going?" Dymitr asks.

"South Chicago," she says. "Where the old steel mill used to be. There's still a factory there."

"And we're going there . . . why?"

She glances at the rearview mirror to see if the driver is paying attention. He is, but when he meets her eyes, he turns up the radio. Music pulses so loud it rattles the car windows.

"You'll see," she says, loud enough for Dymitr to hear her.

They coast along the lakefront with the road to themselves. Moonlight reflects off the water, jagged from the waves. In the distance, the band of light around the top of the Sears Tower glows blue in honor of Father's Day.

"Do you speak Polish?" Dymitr asks her.

"Do you know what a strzyga is?" she asks in return.

Dymitr hesitates, likely for the sake of the driver—but Ala isn't concerned about the driver thinking they're mad, or even less likely, *believing* whatever they say about monsters in the streets of Chicago. Dymitr seems to make the same calculation, because he answers:

"Like a vampire, right?" He grins, and she can't tell whether he's messing with her or not.

"No," she says. "And if that's what you think, we should call this whole thing off *right the fuck now*—"

"Relax," he says. "Yes, I know what they are. Not vampires. Much worse than vampires." He taps the guitar case held between his knees with one finger. "And there's no guitar in here."

That's no surprise, though she wonders what *is* in there.

"Good." She sits back, and chews her thumbnail. A few minutes pass before she remembers that he asked her a question.

"No," she says. "I never learned to speak Polish."

"Your mother didn't teach you?"

Most zmora are women, so it's a safe assumption that her mother would have been the one to teach her. But Ala's mother had resented being forced to learn it by her own mother, who used to slap her knuckles with a ruler if she didn't use the Polish words for things, and she hadn't wanted to inflict the same hardship on her daughter. Ala had grown up with the ache of not knowing it—not knowing where she was from, or what she was, really, as a result.

There are, of course, zmory from other places. They go by other names: lamia in Greek, pesanta in Spanish, dab tsog in Hmong. Even some of her Dryja cousins wear features from other places, their skin umber and russet and sable instead of pale and freckled like her own. But most of them still know how their family came here, and why, and how to speak to the Dryja leaders in their own language. Among them, Ala still feels twinges of loneliness that she tries to ignore. She feels it now, with Dymitr, though he's no zmora.

"No," she says. "She sang to me sometimes, though. One song in particular. A Christmas song—Gdy się Chrystus . . . something."

Dymitr grins.

"'Gdy się Chrystus rodzi'?" he says.

"Maybe. Probably. She used to laugh during the third verse, and I don't know why."

The driver's music fades for a moment between songs, with just a late-night DJ chattering through the speakers. She hears Dymitr singing, his voice creaky but mostly on key: "Powiedzcież wyraźniej co nam czynić trzeba . . . bo my nic nie pojmujemy . . . Ledwo od strachu żyjemy . . ."

Ala can't help but laugh.

"That's it," she says. "Can you translate it?"

"I think . . . 'Say more clearly what we must do, because we don't understand anything. We hardly live . . . from fear.'"

She snorts a little. "Well. She always did have a dark sense of humor." She glances at him. "She was hardly living because of fear, too."

His expression is grave for a moment, and then lightens. "I didn't know your people celebrated Christmas."

"Not everyone who celebrates Christmas believes in it," she points out. "But yes, my mother, like many of my people, was Catholic, likely to the horror of the Holy Order. Some of my people are Protestant, or Jewish, or Muslim, too. But why does that surprise you? Didn't you find that flower in a church?"

"I didn't realize it was planted there in reverence. I'm . . . aware," he says carefully, "that the Holy Order uses religion as a kind of cudgel, as so many others have before them. Their name, even. *Knights.* I just assumed that would turn others away."

"I'm sure it has." Ala shrugs. "But not everyone." She doesn't want to think about it anymore, her mother's creaky voice singing in Polish, the multicolored bulbs on the Christmas tree, so hot they burned her fingers. The times that are lost, now. She changes the subject. "You know, even if you give that flower to me, we still need Baba Jaga to tell us how to cure me. So I'm not getting my hopes up."

"But that's what the song is about," Dymitr says. "The wild hope for . . . restitution. Healing. Despite a total lack of understanding. We could basically just sing it to Baba Jaga, minus the 'gloria's.'" Dymitr turns toward the window to watch the tall buildings of Chicago's downtown pass them by. "You shouldn't lose hope, Ala. Our people never do. We're foolish that way."

"Are you saying I inherited this foolishness?" she says. "That's sort of a relief, actually. I thought it was a condition unique to me."

His smile fades a little, and he nods.

"Keep your hopes up, Aleksja," he says. "Disappointed hopes won't be any worse than what awaits you now."

He has a point.

The driver leaves them in the dark, right off Lake Shore Drive where it follows the bend in the Calumet River and then merges with Harbor Avenue. He gave them both an uneasy look before driving away, and no wonder. The only thing between them and the wasteland of the old steel mill buildings is a newer, redbrick structure. The container factory, still operational.

The only sign that all is not as it should be is the parking lot, packed with cars, and the faint music playing inside.

"What is this place?" Dymitr asks.

"This whole area used to be the steel mill," she says. "For a long time, when immigrants came here, this is where they worked. Now it's all empty except for this factory. Factory by day, anyway—at night, a boxing club run by the Kostkas."

"The Kostkas," Dymitr says. "That's the big strzygi family, right?"

She nods.

"And they come here, why? They love the atmosphere?"

"The city owes this place a debt," she says. "These workers—not just our people, people from all over the world—made the beams that hold up the Sears Tower, the Hancock Building. They poured their sweat into the mill, and none of them got much in return. Derision, mostly, for their trouble. Then when the mill closed, they had nothing."

"Ah," Dymitr says. "So there's a lot of space for magic here."

She nods. "I need you to play along with whatever I say. Even if you don't like it. Can you do that?"

"Yes."

"Let's go, then, or we'll be late," she says. "Listen—there's going to be a lot of . . . different sorts in there. You'll be one of the only humans. If you fuck around, they'll kill you, and I'll let it happen. Got it?"

"Ala," he says, his eyes locking on hers. *"Yes."*

They walk along the first row of cars, which are finer and more polished the closer they get to the door. Ala runs her finger along the hood of an old, well-kept Mercedes—a boxy E-class from the early '90s. Then she shoves her hands in her pockets and walks up to the bouncer.

The bouncer is a Kostka cousin—at least, Ala thinks so. Tall and sturdy in a hot-pink puffer jacket. She snaps bubble gum between her teeth as she eyes Ala.

"It's creature night," she says. "So you should leave your little pet in the car."

She crooks a finger at Dymitr, still not really looking at him. Her fingernail is long and acid green. Strzygi fingernails are matte black, like bird talons, so most strzygi paint them.

"He's oświecony," Ala says. "A cousin."

"We're almost at capacity."

"Well, I was told to hurry, and I'm fighting," Ala says. "Which, last time I checked, means I can bring somebody in to mop up my blood."

The strzyga narrows her eyes at Dymitr. They're inky black. Owl eyes.

"What's in the case?" she asks him.

"A banjo," he replies. "Do you know how to dance the Krakowiak? I could play for you."

The strzyga purses her lips, obviously not amused. But she waves them both toward the door. It's patchy with rust, and it feels hollow when Ala opens it, lighter than it should be.

"Please tell me you don't actually know that dance," Ala says to Dymitr.

"Only if you tell me you aren't actually going to require me to mop up your blood," he says, raising an eyebrow.

She keeps walking. She can't tell him that.

Beyond the door is a cramped entryway, blocked off from the factory floor by flimsy temporary walls and a cluttered desk stacked with paper. Ala walks past it, toward the thrum of the music.

"You can't be serious," Dymitr says. "You're really going to *fight*?"

"How else did you think we were going to get in here?" she says, scowling back at him. "I'm a zmora, and an unimportant one at that. I don't get regular invitations to this place."

Past the temporary walls is a wide-open floor. The equipment—to make the containers, Ala assumes—is pushed up against the walls, a tangle of metal ducts and plates and platforms. She assumes this was done by magic, because there are no outlines on the floor to show where the huge pieces of machinery used to go, and not a scrap of material litters the concrete.

In the middle of the floor where the machinery used to be is a boxing ring, square and blue with black ropes, with a cluster of lights hanging overhead to illuminate it. The rest of the room is dim, with rows of seats arranged around the ring and a wet bar along the far wall.

The room is full of creatures. Ala and Dymitr walk past a cluster of strzygi, recognizable by their yellow, glinting eyes; an alkonost, with her wings tucked against her back and her long, straight hair in a braid; a row of banshees, their big, dark eyes alighting on Dymitr right away, like he called them by name; a handful of czorts, their short, stubby horns uncovered. Ala shivers as they walk past a wraith in the form of a ghostly boy with one skeletal hand.

She spots the chalkboard where the fights are listed, and she's startled to find the word "zmora" at the top. She's the first fight of the night.

"Shit," she says. "I have to find the Pitmaster."

Dymitr is clutching the straps of his guitar case and

emitting a faintly sweet smell, like a dusting of powdered sugar. She thinks it's wariness rather than true fear, and again she wonders at it. She's never met a mortal who could be in a room of strzygi without swallowing his heartbeat.

She leads the way to a tall woman standing next to the boxing ring. She has dark hair, umber skin, and eyes set a little too close together. Her look of appraisal makes Ala stand up a little straighter.

"I'm the zmora," she says, nodding toward the board. "First match."

"Niko said you would surprise me," the woman says, in the hoarse, dry voice common to strzygi. She narrows her eyes. "He had better be right."

The woman picks up a clipboard resting on the bench behind her and checks off the square next to the word "zmora"—everyone knows not to give their names here. Ala stares at the word scribbled next to it, the one for her opponent:

STRZYGA (1).

"Shit," Ala says under her breath, as she steps away from the Pitmaster. "Shit, shit, shit."

"Niko?" Dymitr says, in a low voice. "Did she mean *Nikodem Kostka*?"

"I see my reputation precedes me," a low, amused voice says from behind them.

4

A VALUABLE
INGREDIENT

Nikodem Kostka is startling. Of all the strzygi that Dymitr
has seen—and he's seen more in the last five minutes than
he had in his entire life up to this point—Nikodem is the
one that most closely resembles a bird of prey. His eyes are
a luminous bronze, catching the light like a flame is flickering behind them. He looks at Dymitr like he's spotted a
mouse in the grass to hunt.

"Niko," Ala says, with a nervous smile. "It's not you I'm
fighting, is it?"

"Not tonight," Niko says. "Who have you brought with
you?"

Dymitr wants to back away. Ala's nostrils flare, the tell-
tale sign that he's radiating fear strong enough for her to
smell, maybe even taste. He's glad Niko can't do the same.
Strzygi eat anger, not fear—hence the aggression fostered
by the boxing club.

"His name is Dymitr," Ala says.

"Spoilsport," Niko says to her, grinning. His dark hair
and light brown skin suggest that his father, unlike his
mother, was not Polish—not uncommon among strzygi

in America, where people from all different places have sought refuge . . . even if not all of them found it.

"I don't have time for a protracted argument about names," Ala snaps. "I have to prepare for this." She gestures to the boxing ring behind them. "Thank you for getting me in on such short notice."

"Of course," Niko says. "Though I notice you're still not telling me *why*."

"After." Ala runs her tongue along her bottom lip, obviously a nervous habit. "If I survive."

"Your opponent may be a strzyga, but she's also an idiot. You'll be fine," Niko says. "I'll take care of your guest."

He lays a long-fingered hand on the back of Dymitr's neck, curling his fingertips so Dymitr feels the edge of his thick, sharp fingernails—worn unpainted, so they're as black as claws.

Dymitr tenses. His instinct is to throw Niko off him with as much force as he can muster, but the whole reason Ala is fighting is to get him into a place he wouldn't ordinarily be able to go—so that he can talk to people he wouldn't ordinarily be able to find, let alone engage. He needs to choose his battles.

"Come on," Niko says. "If you sit by me, you'll have a better view."

He presses Dymitr forward, and Dymitr concedes, walking at Nikodem Kostka's side around the edge of the boxing ring to the first row of seats on the other side. He notices, as they pass a crowd of strzygi, that they withdraw from Niko as if he has a plague they don't want to catch. His spare mouth curls into a sharp little smile, scorn and amusement tangled together.

"Sit," Niko says to Dymitr, and he pushes him down.

Dymitr glares at him, but he sits.

Niko grins. "You're so easy to irritate."

"Only by you, it seems."

"Lucky me." Niko sits beside him. "What did you come here looking for, Dymitr?"

"I came to see Ala," Dymitr says.

"Liar." Niko stretches an arm across the back of Dymitr's chair. "Magic is humming around you like an aura. It's making my fingertips prickle." He snaps his fingers, as if to prove it. "But *you* still seem painfully ordinary."

"I don't find it painful to be ordinary."

This startles a laugh from Niko. Dymitr notices that though most of the crowd in the room has settled into the chairs arranged around the boxing ring, the seat to his right, the seat to Niko's left, and the seats behind them are all empty.

"I have a question for you," Dymitr says, in a low voice, leaning closer to Niko's ear.

Niko stills, staring at him with his eyes like lit embers.

"Why do your own people fear you?" Dymitr asks.

Niko smiles, but Dymitr doesn't know how he would have answered, because a woman is walking into the center of the boxing ring. She's freckled, with big, sad eyes, and wears a black gown that makes her look like a soprano in an opera. A moment later, when she clasps her hands over her belly and begins to sing, he thinks that effect was deliberate.

She's a banshee—that's the most frequently used terminology, at least. Her voice makes that obvious enough, but he isn't sure what purpose she serves here. As far as he knows, banshees feast on sorrow the way the zmory feast on fear, and they have the power to provoke sorrow, too, drawing it from the deepest parts of a person at will. These three types of *creatures*—the zmora, the strzyga, and the llorona, or banshee—represent a trifecta, each consuming one of the primary negative emotions. The picture his Chicago informant painted was one of a kind of underground network of emotion farming, of which the Crow Theater, the boxing ring, and the banshees' small franchise of hospice facilities was just a fraction. The families at the head of those "farms" are the Dryjas, the Kostkas, and the O'Connor-Vasquezes, respectively. This particular banshee has auburn hair and freckles he assumes come from the O'Connors, but the women across the boxing ring, with their dark eyes and shiny black hair, seem to favor the Vasquezes.

But they wouldn't have invited a banshee to sing as a prelude to a boxing match if all she could do was make everyone feel sad. As her unearthly voice climbs to a piercing high, he grits his teeth, unsure what to expect. She soars over the highest note, and it vibrates in Dymitr's skull, as if it's turned him into glass that's about to break. And break he does, silently, the walls he's placed around his emotions crumbling all at once. Feeling spills through him, rage and sorrow and terror, frustration and regret and dread. The singing banshee fixes her stare on him, and he closes his eyes, his hands in fists against his knees.

"Well," Niko says, as the song comes to a gentle close. "That was interesting."

He sounds sluggish, almost like he's drunk. Dymitr doesn't answer. He's too busy reconstructing what the banshee destroyed. By the time he gathers himself, the fight is starting.

"Almost no one bet on her, you know," Niko says, nodding toward Ala, now ducking under the ropes and looking even more wan than usual. "Zmory aren't known for being good fighters. Good at escaping, more like. Or fucking with you."

Ala peels off her zip-up and hangs it over the ropes. Under it, she wears the plain gray T-shirt from Toil and Trouble, the one with the sleeves sawed off. She looks broader here than she did there, the bright light showcasing definition in her shoulders. She takes off the rings she wears and tucks them in her pocket.

Her opponent is a Kostka strzyga with a nose that looks like it's been broken more than once. Her long, dark hair is in a braid, and she has a faint overbite that makes her mouth look like a beak.

"What do you actually know about Ala, beyond the fact that she's a zmora?" Niko asks.

"What do *you* know?"

"I know a person isn't a species."

Dymitr frowns. "Do you think I'm not aware of that?"

"You might try to be," Niko says. "But the truth is, you've met too few of her kind to know what about her is zmora and what about her is just her." He tilts his head. "Am I wrong?"

Ala faces the strzyga—who's fighting under the name "Teresa," though Dymitr is sure that's a pseudonym, given how paranoid everyone seems to be about giving their name—and somewhere in the warehouse, a bell goes off. Teresa launches herself at Ala with enthusiasm, all the speed and strength of her kind evident in the sure, fast movement.

Ala, in response, simply . . . shrinks.

Of course, she can't *actually* shrink—zmory aren't shapeshifters—but the illusion is so perfect that she appears to. A child stands in her place, small and thin with scabby knees.

"Pretty please," the child says, her voice reedy. "Don't hurt me, please!"

The strzyga falters, blinking at the child, who steps toward her with arms outstretched. The momentary hesitation costs her, because as the child moves, it seems to grow, stretching grotesquely until Ala is standing in front of her again, punching her in the face.

The crowd gasps as one, and Ala slips away.

"You're not wrong. I haven't met many zmory," Dymitr says, then. "So tell me about her."

"Well, most zmory aren't quite that good at illusions," Niko says with a laugh.

Teresa stumbles back, the velvet ropes catching her, and licks blood from the corner of her mouth. Ala grins at her, and Teresa lunges, her face shifting into that of a bird.

Every strzyga has a sowa form, an owl-like shape that they can move into at will. Teresa's is a snowy owl, the rim of her yellow eyes stark, only a hint of black dappling the top of her head. Wings explode from her back, wide and white, and her fingernails grow into true talons. With a screech, she launches herself into the air, lands on Ala, and bites down at the juncture between Ala's neck and shoulder.

"Ala helped a friend of mine once," Niko says casually, like they aren't both watching Ala's shirt turn bright red with blood. "He was fighting off some Holy Order scum, defending a young zmora—one of the Dryja cousins, I think—and though Aleksja was young at the time, she had this skill—"

Ala screams, and grabs Teresa's wing, wrenching it to the side hard enough to make Teresa release her. Then she disappears.

It's a far more advanced illusion than it appears, Dymitr thinks. It requires Ala to re-create the details of the boxing ring exactly, but without her body inside of it, and to project those details not just to Teresa, but to everyone in the room.

He's never seen anything like it.

"She produces extremely detailed illusions," Niko continues. "In this case, she made the Knight think he was covered in something—spiders, I think—and he was so distracted he gave my friend a chance to run away, young Dryja cousin in tow. She saved his life."

Teresa, her face still an owl's, looks around the arena, confused by the sudden disappearance of her opponent. Dymitr only has time to observe a faint depression in the boxing ring floor and a shadow Ala didn't quite manage to hide when Ala reappears midair, jumping on Teresa's back and wrapping one strong arm around her neck.

Teresa chokes and thrashes, but Ala locks her arms and clamps her knees around Teresa's ribs. Teresa rams her back into one of the posts at the corner of the arena, and Ala grunts with pain, but doesn't release her.

"Fucking—zmora—bitch!" Teresa chokes.

"My friend didn't survive much longer than that—the Knights are too relentless," Niko goes on. "But Ala gave him a few weeks he wouldn't otherwise have had. Bravery and kindness create a debt, and I repay debts, even if they belonged to my fallen friend."

Teresa falls back, Ala still wrapped around her like a squid. She falls in such a way that Ala is trapped beneath her; her hold breaks from the force of the fall, and Teresa elbows her hard in the side. Ala rolls away, and everything goes dark.

This trick, Dymitr recognizes. Klara pulled it on him at the Crow. It seems simple compared to what Ala did last, but then, she just caught an elbow to the ribs. He hears scuffling, a groan, and then the illusion of blackness disappears, like the trip of a light switch. He sees Teresa pinned to the mat in the middle of the boxing ring, with her arm wrenched behind her and Ala's knee in her back.

Teresa's owl face shifts back into her human one, and she slaps the mat, yielding. Ala releases her. Blood streaks her shoulder, but there's a satisfied look on her face.

Niko smiles, with teeth.

"I just made a disgusting amount of money," he says to Dymitr. "I bet on her."

Dymitr's stated purpose in being at the fight is to clean up Ala afterward, so that's what he does. He asks Niko for a first aid kit, and though Niko doesn't respond, he turns up with one a few minutes later, setting it down next to Ala on the bench where she sits, recovering. He says something about getting her a beer, and strides away.

Everywhere he goes, the crowd parts for him.

"I can handle it," Ala says to Dymitr as he crouches beside her to bandage her wound.

"I'm sure you can," he replies. "But we're still keeping up appearances, *cousin*."

Rolling her eyes, she tugs the collar of her T-shirt aside to bare the strzyga's bite. He's familiar with this procedure: he sanitizes his hands, pulls on a pair of latex gloves, and rips open an antiseptic wipe.

Ala raises her eyebrows at him.

"You tend to a lot of bite wounds in your line of work?" she says. "Come to think of it, what is your line of work?"

"I'm unemployed at the moment," he answers. "But as it happens, I grew up with a half-wild dog and a sister who couldn't help but provoke it to bite her."

He thinks of Elza sitting on the kitchen counter with her arm stuck out, her legs swinging. She didn't understand, even after the third incident, that she shouldn't try to take Borys's bone away.

"German shepherd?" Ala guesses.

"Pomeranian," he says, dabbing her wound with the antiseptic. She laughs, and for just a moment, she's Elza in the yellow-tiled kitchen, laughing at one of his horrible jokes.

"If you'd ever met a Pomeranian, you wouldn't think it was so funny," he says, and he presses a clean square of gauze to the juncture of her shoulder and neck. She holds it there while he fastens it with tape.

She seems tired, sweaty, and bruised, but otherwise unharmed. He comes to his feet just as the Pitmaster approaches them.

"You've been summoned," the strzyga says, tossing her curly black hair over one shoulder to gesture to the back corner. Dymitr can't see what she's trying to show them, but zmora eyes must be sharper, because Ala nods.

"You and the human both," the strzyga adds, without looking at Dymitr.

"Fantastic," Ala says under her breath, once the Pitmaster is out of hearing distance.

"What is it?" he says.

"Good news for you, I think," Ala says. "The head of the Kostka family wants to meet you."

Lidia Kostka looks middle-aged, which for a strzyga means she must be very old indeed. Her hair is copper in color and styled in a finger-waved bob straight from the 1920s—and she may have been wearing it that way since then. Her face is a sickly color, and her eyebrows are so fine and pale she almost seems to lack them entirely. If not for her eyes, she would resemble a wealthy woman from another time—but her *eyes*. They're bright yellow and piercing as a shriek. They focus on him from the moment he steps into the room, and he feels them like heat.

Without thinking, he slides a hand into his pocket to touch the fern flower, safely wrapped in paper. They have one day before it's no longer useful, and not to use it would be a criminal waste of magic—a waste of the pain that Dymitr gave to attain it.

The Pitmaster led them here from the boxing ring: away from the factory floor, to the end of a bare hallway where a line of creatures waits for the bathroom, and through a hatch in the floor guarded by a hulking man with a sword who seems to be completely human.

There was a network of rooms and hallways under the factory, which probably shouldn't have surprised Dymitr as much as it did. The strzygi wouldn't have chosen it as a haunt if it were merely a factory.

The room in which he now finds himself is dim, but elaborately decorated. The far wall is covered in a screen of delicate Art Deco metalwork that he recognizes as distinctly "Chicago" in feeling. Low navy-gray sofas are positioned around the room. A marble-top bar stretches along the right wall. There are little lamps with bright red shades positioned here and there, spots of brightness in the dark. One such lamp stands on a table beside Lidia Kostka, making her hair appear even redder.

She stays seated as Ala and Dymitr approach her, as do the other Kostka cousins lounging around her. Dymitr notices Niko slipping into the room behind them and sidling up to the bar, casual, as if he were already planning on coming here and the timing is just coincidence.

Almost all the strzygi in the room are women, and that's no surprise. Dymitr's father told him that Chicago was a city ruled by monsters, and all those monsters were women—strzyga, zmora, and llorona, each a legend of wronged women, sinful women, mysterious women. Tragic and powerful figures, all, not to be underestimated.

Lidia looks Ala up and down, and smiles, faintly.

"We've never had a zmora in our ring before," Lidia says to her, her voice creaky and weak. The room goes quiet when she speaks, as if everyone is straining to hear her. "I hope you don't mind my curiosity about you, Aleksja Dryja."

"Of course not, proszę pani," Ala says, stumbling a little over the term of respectful address.

Lidia laughs, a wheezing little thing.

"That word falls out of your mouth like you're spitting

out bad food," she says. "Did your mother tell you *any-thing* about your origins?"

Ala stiffens beside Dymitr.

"She came here several years after World War Two," she says. "I don't know exactly why."

"Ah," Lidia says. "A relatively recent addition to our little community, then."

"Not that recent." Ala sounds terse. She's taller in reality than she is in Dymitr's mind. Maybe one seventy-five, or however she says it in feet and inches.

"The first of us came earlier," Lidia says. "After the November Uprising. Do you know about the November Uprising?"

She softens over the words like she's speaking to a child. Dymitr wonders how old Ala really is. Older than she looks, surely. Zmory age slowly—slower even than strzygi.

"A little," Ala says.

"So, no, then."

Ala flushes, and that's when Dymitr pieces it together: Lidia is making Ala angry on purpose, not simply to embarrass her but also to feed on her emotions. At this point it must be an instinct, so deeply ingrained that she might not even know she's doing it.

"Others had taken our country and broken it into pieces," Lidia says, and all around the room are murmurs of assent, of recollection, or simply echoes of appreciation, it's hard to say. "They ignored even the smallest bits of our sovereignty that we had carved out for ourselves.

This affected our people as much as mortals. And so some of our kind joined the resistance effort. We fought Russian governance, and we lost. So we fled here. We were not the first—or the last—to flee our country to survive. Sometimes it was because we weren't human, but sometimes it was because we were too human—the wrong religion, during the war, or perhaps the wrong political affiliation, after it. It's interesting to me that your mother didn't tell you why she had to leave."

Lidia tucks a lock of her red hair behind her ear.

"She thought of it as a kindness," Ala says. "She wanted me to have a fresh start in the world. So she didn't do to me anything that she hated being done to herself. Unfortunately, that included teaching me certain things. Her history. Her language."

"I see." Lidia looks unimpressed, but she doesn't provoke Ala further. Instead, she asks, "And what became of her?"

"A curse killed her," Ala says bluntly. "It then passed to her younger sister, to my cousin, and to me, in turn. I came here in pursuit of a cure."

"You came to a strzyga for a cure to a curse?" Lidia smiles. "You are aware, of course, that we can do only small magic, like you?"

It's just a quick look that passes between Ala and Dymitr, but it's enough to catch Lidia's attention. Before Ala can answer her, Lidia is coming to her feet and moving toward them.

Lidia is the same height as Ala, but spare as a wraith,

willow-limbed and delicate. She folds her hands together in front of her, and stands before Dymitr, her head tilted up so she can look him in the eye.

"You are no Dryja cousin," she says to him.

"No, I'm not," he replies.

"What is it you carry, boy?" she asks. She reaches out and pinches the edge of his jacket pocket, but doesn't reach in. "I saw you touch it as you came in, and now your hand bears its imprint." She hooks a finger around his thumb, and lifts his hand, as a hunter might display a kill to a room of peers. Dymitr can't see what she sees, but one of Lidia's companions on the sofa stands, blinking wonderingly at Dymitr. She's the banshee from before, he realizes. The one who sang at the beginning of the fight.

"I see it," the banshee says softly. Her speaking voice is as musical as her singing voice was, low and clear as a bell. "He was already incandescent with sorrow, but now—"

"Yes, I'm sure," Lidia says dryly. She releases his hand. "Let me guess. You have something that can help our friend Aleksja here. But you don't know how to use it. So you likely went to the oldest zmora first, and when she didn't help you . . ." Lidia taps her own chest. "Second-best option."

"Actually," he says, "I'm looking for someone older than any of you."

The hint of amusement curling Lidia's mouth disappears. He didn't even know it was there until it was gone. She was tickled at the idea that they would come seeking her because of her wisdom, born of age, but instead . . . he's revealed that she's just a means to an end. A severe miscalculation on his part.

"Baba Jaga," Lidia says, turning away. She sits down on the sofa again.

"I thought, if anyone might know how to contact her," he says, "it would be you, proszę pani."

"Take note, Aleksja. That's how you say it," Lidia says, sliding an arm along the back of the sofa. "I'm not buying it, boy. If I'm correct in thinking it's the fern flower that you carry—and given the time of year, it seems likely— then you would have had more luck asking the wraith who guarded it. You came here because you had no idea where else to go."

A severe miscalculation indeed.

Dymitr looks at Ala, as if she'll know something he doesn't. She sighs.

"What gift can we offer you?" Ala says. "To communicate our gratitude for your help, before we even receive it?"

Lidia taps her fingers on the back of the sofa. Her fingernails are filed into neat ovals and painted deep red. She glances at the strzyga to her left, who leans forward to murmur something in her ear.

"A fine suggestion," Lidia says to her. She looks at Ala and Dymitr again. "You have a valuable ingredient you want my help with. So you will supply *me* with a valuable ingredient, and I will consider helping you."

"An ingredient," Dymitr repeats.

"A gift born of pain," Lidia says. "A powerful item to aid in healing, if offered willingly."

"A gift born of pain. You mean a fingernail?" Ala says. "You want me to pull out one of my own fingernails?"

Dymitr remembers, suddenly, the cemetery a few miles outside of the town where he grew up. The graves dug up, the corpses untouched in their coffins except for their absent fingernails and teeth. Witches, his grandmother said. A gift willingly given was twice as powerful, but one unwillingly given would still do.

"You, him, whichever," Lidia says, shrugging. "Do this, and your sacrifice will create a substance with strong magic. That's my price."

She looks from Ala to Dymitr with her eyebrows raised, expectant. The strzyga who offered the suggestion is grinning. There's a narrow gap between her front teeth that would be charming if Dymitr didn't hate her so much.

"I'll need a knife," Dymitr says. "And some pliers."

5

A MURDER MOST FOUL

Ala feels as if she ought to object, like someone reaching for their wallet at the end of dinner even if they don't intend to open it. But Dymitr doesn't seem to expect it. He meets Lidia's eyes and waits.

For some reason, Ala isn't surprised when Niko steps out of the shadows near the bar and tips his head to Lidia in something like a bow.

"Babcia," he says.

"Call me your grandmother again and I'll cut off your head, zemsta," Lidia says, but she's smiling a little. Ala doesn't recognize the word "zemsta," but it makes the room smell like warm honey, like wariness. All the strzygi at once, reacting.

"My apologies," Niko says. "But I wanted to offer to do the honors myself. It can be a nasty business, this . . . fingernail pulling. You shouldn't lower yourself to it."

Lidia appears to consider this for a moment.

"Please," she says. Niko smiles, and walks out of the room, presumably to fetch a pair of pliers.

Dymitr, for his part, seems unfazed. Ala can't detect much more than a faint whiff of sugar-sweet anticipation from him. He stands near the bar as the bartender—a czort with blunt black horns poking out of his hair—sterilizes a penknife using a cigarette lighter. Niko turns up a few minutes later with needle-nose pliers in hand and carries both pliers and penknife over to Dymitr.

"May I sit?" Dymitr says to Lidia, gesturing to the empty chair across from her. It's tucked under one of the low tables. At her nod, he pulls it out and sits, holding his hand beneath the red lamp.

Lidia slides down the sofa, closer to the banshee, and points at the place she just occupied, her eyes on Niko. She looks like she's getting ready to watch a movie or a dance performance, her legs crossed at the ankle and her hands folded over her belly. Casual.

"Why the knife?" Niko asks Dymitr, as the latter presses his hand flat on the table and positions the blade over his pinkie finger.

"If you just yank out a fingernail with pliers, you can damage the nail bed permanently," Dymitr says. "I'm going to . . . loosen it."

"Wait," Niko says, before Dymitr can dig in. He gets up and reaches over the bar for a bottle of amber liquor. Whiskey. He pours a shot of it and carries it over to the table. When he sets it down in front of Dymitr, he bends low, close to his ear. "Some mercy for you."

"How good of you," Dymitr says, a hint of sourness in his voice. But he takes the shot, and picks up the knife again.

Ala considers turning away, but as Dymitr presses the blade steadily into his own fingernail, she finds she can't.

Bright red blood bubbles up around his fingernail as he traces its outline. His hand, his breaths, his eyes—they're all steady.

"I feel like you have more than a passing familiarity with this procedure," Niko comments.

"My little sister slammed her fingernail in a door once," Dymitr says. "It was half on, half off. We were in the middle of nowhere and she needed it gone . . . so my father did exactly this. My job was . . . to hold her still."

He sounds tense, his words punctuated by bursts of breath, but he seems to have a high pain tolerance for a human.

"Sounds traumatic," Niko says.

"She bit me." Dymitr sets down the penknife to tap a silvery scar on his left forearm. It's jagged but curved, like teeth. "Time for the pliers."

He smells nervous now, like peaches, like strawberries. Ala moves closer without meaning to, drawn in by his fear.

Niko positions the pliers over the tip of Dymitr's bloody finger. Their eyes meet.

Dymitr nods, and Niko pulls.

Ala can't stand to look, then. She flinches and turns away at the sound of Dymitr's yell, muffled by his wrist. She wonders if he'll leave a bite there to match his little sister's.

She turns back in time to see Niko holding Dymitr's fingernail aloft, still pinched in the pliers. Dymitr, meanwhile, is hunched over, trembling. Blood spatters the floor beneath him.

Niko offers him a handkerchief, but his eyes are on Ala's. "Cover your eyes," he says to her. "Now."

Ala has just enough time to bring her arm up to her head when Niko flicks his wrist, sending the fingernail flying. It's just reached its apex when he says, in his rough, deep voice, *"Promienny."*

A brilliant light explodes from the fingernail, and Ala shuts her eyes. A moment later she feels a hand on her wrist.

"Keep them shut," Niko's voice says, and he yanks her toward the door.

She knows only by her nose that Dymitr is with them, the scent of his fear more potent than she's detected so far. She smells mildew, too, and she knows she's in the hall-way just outside. She stumbles after Niko, her wrist still captive to his stern grip and her shoulder aching from the strzyga bite she got during the fight.

"You can open them now!" Niko says. "And I'd recommend an illusion in—Well, now."

Ala's vision is crowded with dark patches from her brief glimpse of the fingernail, but when she looks over her shoulder, she sees a few strzygi toppling out of the room where they just were, squinting. She doesn't have time to refine an illusion, to master its details. She just creates an image of three moving shadows climbing the stairs, and another three shadows running down the hallway to their left. Niko leads them down the hallway on the right.

She gets brief glimpses of the rooms they pass: another sitting room; a smaller boxing ring stacked with pads, for practice; an office with a padded chair and a closed laptop; a supply closet full of liquor bottles; a wine cellar. The creaky wood beneath her shoes gives way to plain concrete again, and she smells rot as well as mildew—the lake. She heard once that they closed the beaches because the *E. coli* levels of the lake got too high, causing her to wonder just how high they were on an average weekend, and why anyone would *ever* swim in Lake Michigan while that information was readily available—

Dymitr holds his bloody hand against his chest, and his guitar case bumps against his shoulders with each running footstep. He looks pale and clammy, but more focused than Ala feels, than she thinks she could ever be with a pack of strzygi on her heels.

Niko hits a door at the end of the hallway shoulder first, and it opens to a set of cracked and mossy stairs, and the taste of the night air, which Ala picks apart without even thinking about it: mud, garbage, exhaust, grass, gravel. Without even knowing if there's anyone behind them, she sends illusory figures tumbling in every direction, like ants spilling out of a ruined anthill. Dymitr blinks at them, and she grabs his elbow, dragging him along.

"Don't get distracted," she snaps, and they both chase Niko across the parking lot.

Where a group of strzygi wait for them.

The first time Ala's mother ever talked to her about the curse, she had been afflicted by it for a year already, seeing phantoms every morning where there were none, rambling about snow getting in her boots even though it was August, and making Ala's aunt—not really her aunt, but her mother's closest friend—fuss over her until her mind cleared, typically sometime around noon.

Her mother sat at the kitchen table, which was rickety and round and salvaged from an alley a few blocks away from them. Ala had wedged a piece of cardboard under one of the legs to keep it from wobbling, but it wobbled anyway. Her mother stirred honey into her tea—chamomile, to relax her—with a dazed expression. Ala cradled a mug of coffee to her chest and worked on that day's crossword.

"I know how it seems," her mother said, still stirring her tea. Her eyes were focused on the center of the table. "Like I am going mad."

"Mom, that isn't—"

"You are very careful not to say so." Her mother's eyes were a dull blue. Almost gray, sometimes, in certain lights. "You are too careful of me, I think. Do you think I can't tell that you are afraid of me now?"

She sniffed, as if to make her point.

"You smell like a fucking bakery," she said, and Ala's face warmed. She went on: "So. Let us get the truth out there. They are not delusions. I know they aren't real, when I'm inside them."

"Oh," Ala said, setting her pencil down. "What . . . what is it you see, exactly?"

Her mother shrugged. Her nightgown slipped off her shoulder, exposing a freckled collarbone and the little round scar on her upper arm from the smallpox vaccine.

She swept her palm across the center of the table, and a scene appeared. Ala's mother was gifted with small, detailed illusions that reminded her of dioramas or model train sets. She couldn't immerse you in them, but she could show the whole picture at once, something that always made Ala a little envious.

On the table before them was what looked like a Christmas landscape: a little house on a snow-covered hill that poked up from a dark forest. It was nighttime, and the moonlight turned the snow blue-white.

As Ala watched, two men on horseback rode through the trees toward the house. Only one light was on inside it, a warm and unsteady glow that reminded Ala of a lantern or a hearth fire. She could see one of the riders by its light when he passed in front of the house.

Even though he was small, no larger than a china doll, she could still see that his palms were stained the deep red of the Holy Order.

The Knight dismounted and drew his sword, which was fascinating to watch from this distance. The hilt was buried in his flesh, like his spine was bulging from his body. He had to dig into his skin to loosen it, which he did with the ease of someone who had done it a thousand times before. But she could see the agony of it nonetheless, his red-stained hands shuddering, his tiny teeth gritted.

He drew it, then dragged it across his arm hard enough to draw blood, and said something in Polish that Ala didn't understand.

Then the birds came. They were crows, but larger and fiercer than their natural brethren, cursed to serve the will of the one who summoned them. In miniature as they were, they reminded Ala of a swarm of flies, black and clustered together. The other Knight broke a window with an axe, and the birds flew into the open space he created, filling the house with wings and beaks.

Ala saw a face in the window. A woman's face, her hair bedraggled from sleep. She pounded on the glass, and Ala couldn't understand what she said, but she assumed it was a plea for help. A moment later, her face disappeared beneath the windowsill.

Ala lifted her gaze to her mother's. The tiny illusion disappeared.

"I see only the Holy Order," her mother said. "Again and again, as they kill our kind, our strzygi brethren, our wraith cousins, everyone. It's like watching a horror movie I can't look away from. Those swords. Their empty eyes. Their unnatural magic. Half-souled beasts."

She bowed her head. Her cheeks looked sunken.

"It is killing me," she said. "Just as it killed my mother. Just as it will kill you, one day. This curse lives in our blood, Ala, and it cannot be stopped."

Ala sometimes wished her mother could soften things for her, just a little. But she wouldn't—or more accurately, she couldn't. She didn't know how to live in a world that wasn't straightforward. She had, for all her zmora talents, no patience for illusions.

Ala stopped doing the crossword after that.

There's a breath of stillness as Niko spots the strzygi who are waiting for them. He slows, keeping Ala and Dymitr behind him.

"Now, now," he says. "Let's all be reasonable."

Ala sees something out of the corner of her eye that looks almost like one of her illusions. But she sent them running toward the river, the lake, the nearby road. This shadow is stationary, standing too far away to be more than a dark shape even to Ala's sharp eyes.

"Reasonable?" one of the strzygi spits. "You just attacked—"

"I did no such thing," Niko argues.

"He has the *fern flower*," one of the others says. "Take it from him and dispose of him!"

Niko tilts his head as if he's considering this. Ala sees movement again, this time from the shadow by the water. The shine of a knife. A sharp jerking movement, both familiar and sinister in its familiarity.

"No, I don't think I will," Niko says, but Ala barely hears him over the distant flutter, the croaking call that coasts over the sound of the waves, the cars, the low music of the boxing ring.

She knows that sound.

She raises her head to see a dark cloud of movement above her. And then she tastes it in the back of her throat, feather and blood, one of the visions that haunts her again and again thanks to the curse that courses through her veins. In it, a flock of enchanted crows summoned by Knights of the Holy Order descend on the house in the country. They surround a woman in her living room as she pounds on her window.

They peck out her eyes.

Ala drops to her knees on the pavement right as the birds descend. It's instinct more than analysis that creates the illusion: she sends dozens of shimmering lights across the parking lot, little glinting things that will draw the birds' attention. She hears screams, and something clatters to the ground beside her: the needle-nose pliers that Niko used to pull out Dymitr's fingernail.

She grabs them, maintaining the illusions, and stabs upward as a bird dives at her head. Dymitr is nowhere to be seen—probably ran at the first sign of danger, not that she can blame him. Beside her, Niko has shifted, huge black wings dappled with white stretching wide to lift him from the ground, his bronze eyes unchanged, though his face is now that of a stygian owl, horned and fierce.

Ala swats at a bird that flaps too close to her ear, and hits another one with the side of the pliers, hard enough to knock it off course. Everywhere is the croak and caw of crows, and the glint of sleek black feathers in the moonlight.

Across the parking lot she hears a clang as the bouncer disappears inside the factory, slamming the door behind her. The other strzygi have either gone inside or scattered, leaving only Niko and Ala to fend off the flock—the fuck-ing *murder* of enchanted, bloodthirsty crows.

She lets instinct guide her, and sends shadows sprinting in every direction, like ripples radiating out from the focal point of her. The crows collide as they pursue different versions of her, and she stabs another one with the pliers. Beside her, Niko has his wicked sharp beak buried in the throat of one bird while he snatches another out of the air.

But there are still dozens more where those came from, and the air is thick with black feathers. Though she doesn't pause to look at him, she can see Niko in her periphery, a fiercer fighter than she's ever seen; he dives and claws with ruthless efficiency, felling four birds to her one. She spares a second to wonder about Dymitr, her clawless hands dig-ging into a crow's inexplicably moist feathers, when an ar-row whizzes past her face and buries in a distant bird's belly.

She hears another arrow, and another one, and finally looks over her shoulder to see Dymitr with a bow and quiver. Seems she's finally solved the mystery of what he's carrying instead of a guitar. He draws from the quiver again and again with the ease of someone who mastered the art a long time ago. She takes note of the focus in his eyes for just a moment before she stoops to yank an arrow out of a fallen bird, then wields it like a knife, slashing at the next one to dive at her.

A minute or so later—thanks in no small part to Dy-mitr's rapid and accurate projectiles—the birds have thinned. Niko lands on light feet and shifts back, wiping his sleeve over his blood-soaked mouth.

"Come on!" he shouts, and he runs toward one of the cars in the parking lot, an impractical cloth-top Jeep Wrangler with duct tape patching up one of the back windows.

Ala spares a look at Dymitr, who is now lowering his bow, but there's no discussion. They both follow.

6

AN INTERLUDE

Niko reaches across Ala, sitting in the passenger seat, to take a pack of cigarettes out of the glove box. One sticky, bloody hand on the wheel, he opens the pack, tucks a cigarette between his lips, and reaches for the lighter in the cup holder. Ala gets there first, rolling her eyes as she sparks the flame to life for him.

He leaves red fingerprints on the edge of the cigarette that he tastes every time he takes a drag, but it doesn't matter. His mouth is full of the remnants of bird anyway. It's disgusting, but he's good at redirecting his thoughts. He has to be, doing what he does with his time.

The car isn't his. He's borrowing it from his mortal cousin, Janek, who doesn't appear to realize that he lives in one of the chillier cities in America. He also installed an aboveground pool in his backyard a few years back. Niko has an assortment of stupid cousins like Janek—when a strzyga has a son, he usually comes out human, which is why there are so few like Niko in existence. So on the fringes of the Kostka family, there are always a handful of men, relegated to less central roles such as "bouncer" and "bodyguard" and "maintenance worker."

The window on his side of the monstrosity is unzipped, letting in cool air and the sound of cars rushing past them, traveling in the opposite direction. There are always people out, even when night is turning to morning, as it's now doing.

"Well," he says, once he feels calm. "That was a lot of birds."

Ala and Dymitr both make the same sound: a little grunt of assent.

"Anyone care to explain *how* we were just attacked by that many birds?" Niko asks, with the tone of a kindergarten teacher nagging a classroom of unfocused students.

"They were summoned," Ala says. "I saw the one who did it."

"You saw them?" Dymitr replies.

"Not . . . in detail," Ala says. "But I saw someone standing near the river, and they . . ." She frowns, and makes a jerking motion with her arm. "I'm not sure what they were doing."

"Blood ritual," Dymitr says.

Niko considers this for a moment, then guides the car into a gas station. The gas tank is full, but he believes in safe driving, and what he's about to do doesn't qualify.

He flicks his cigarette out the window and fumbles under his seat for the knife he keeps there. Once it's secure in his hand, he reaches back and holds the blade to Dymitr's throat.

"What the fuck?" Ala says.

Dymitr goes still.

"How do you know that?" Niko says.

Dymitr knows a flock of enchanted birds was summoned by a blood ritual, which means he possesses more than basic knowledge about the Holy Order, the only ones who do such rituals. Bloody, masochistic rituals that force the sacrifice that magic requires.

He can feel Dymitr's skin burning into the backs of his fingers where they're curled around the knife handle. The unsteady movement of his swallow.

"You know a great deal about the Holy Order," Niko says, when Dymitr doesn't respond. "There's no point in denying it."

"I'm not denying it," Dymitr says. "I'm just not sure why it's any of your business what I know."

"Considering I just saved your life from a pack of strzygi that would have murdered you for the flower you're keeping in your pocket, I'd say it's a little bit my business."

"I don't recall asking you to do that."

"Oh, for fuck's sake," Ala says, slamming her hand down on the dashboard. She twists around to look at Dymitr. "Do you *really* think that you can get an audience with Baba Jaga without answering anyone's questions about you?"

Dymitr stares back at her, steady.

"The only way mortal men know that much about the Holy Order is because they've summoned them to kill one of us," Ala says, her voice going uncharacteristically soft. "Please tell me that's not how you know them."

"Of course not," Dymitr says, and Ala relaxes a fraction.

Niko's arm is starting to ache from holding the knife to Dymitr's throat, so he lets it drop, but doesn't put it away.

Dymitr chews on his lower lip. He still has a handkerchief tied around his right pinkie. His bow and arrows are back in his guitar case, leaning against his knee.

"I want an audience with Baba Jaga," Dymitr says, "because I want to destroy a member of the Holy Order, and I lack the ability to do it on my own."

Niko wasn't sure what he was going to say, but he didn't expect . . . *that*.

"Why?" Ala says, quiet.

"You can choose to believe me, or you can choose not to believe me," Dymitr says. "But that's all I'm going to tell you, regardless."

Niko stares at Dymitr, aware of the tight feeling of blood dried on his hands, of the smell of sweat emanating from his skin, of the particular sensations of Dymitr's anger—subtle, too subtle for most strzygi to be interested in, but present nonetheless. He considers, again, why he bothered to stop the others from killing this man. As a rule, Niko doesn't involve himself in Kostka affairs. His own role is clearly defined. He was set apart before he took his oath, and he's set apart even further now—one of them, but not one of them.

But there's something about him, Dymitr. A kind of clarity that most mortals—hell, most *people*—don't possess. He didn't hesitate for a moment before volunteering himself for pain in Ala's place. Didn't seem afraid while standing in Lidia's private lounge, going head-to-head with the leader of a centuries-old strzyga family. He feels, in short, like someone who's on a mission, and Niko finds himself wanting to know what that mission is.

Without a word, Niko drops his knife in the cup holder and shifts the car into drive.

"As it happens," Niko says, "I know where we should go next."

"*We?*" Ala says. "You're helping us now?"

"I thought that was implied." Niko pulls back onto the street. "How did you get so good with a bow, Dymitr?"

"My grandmother taught me," Dymitr says, which startles a laugh out of Niko.

"Quite a mental image," he says. "Some old babushka at target practice."

"If you met her," Dymitr says, looking out the window, "you wouldn't dare call her that."

Niko smiles. "I'm sure."

"I have to go," Ala says suddenly. Her voice is hard and urgent. "Right now." Her eyes are on the dashboard clock, and then on the rearview mirror, where the glow around the horizon suggests sunrise. "The curse. It surges at dawn. I'll take a taxi back—"

"To the north side?" Dymitr says. "You can't make it all the way back there before dawn."

"Well, great, then I guess I'm fucked!"

"I'll take us to a safe place," Niko says, in what he hopes is a reassuring tone. "Just . . . hold on, okay?"

The Peaceful Journeys Hospice Care Center stands in the southwest side of the city, between a budget grocery store with rogue shopping carts rolling through the parking lot and a Denny's that was obviously retrofitted into an old White Castle. The logo on the hospice center sign is that of a woman in a long dress, her hair streaming behind her, which is a nod to the center's owners: the O'Connor-Vasquez family. Banshees. Well, the Irish O'Connors would say ben síde, and the Mexican Vasquezes would prefer llorona—weepers—but it amounts to the same thing.

They own a small chain of hospice care facilities, actually. And a handful of funeral homes. The O'Connor-Vasquezes seem to know a truth that the Kostkas and the Dryjas don't, which is that there's plenty of food to go around. They eat sorrow, and the harvest is always plentiful. They simply position themselves where they're most likely to remain sated without effort.

Some of them seek out variation, of course. He's seen some of their number at rehabilitation facilities, cemeteries, and even poetry readings at college open mic nights. But they always return to places like these, where death is close at hand. Maybe that's why they got the reputation they did, as portents of doom, or even prophets in their own right. As far as Niko knows, that's nonsense, but mortals are always devising nonsense.

The building is straightforward. White and rectangular, with a circle drive large enough to accommodate an ambulance—or a hearse. Concrete planters by the automatic doors hold clumps of purple and yellow pansies.

When they step inside, the first thing he hears is gentle elevator music. A saxophone. A chime.

"Welcome to—Oh," the young woman at the front desk says, her eyes dropping to Niko's bloodstained shirt, his streaked hands. If she were mortal, she would call the police. But her wide, round eyes skip from Niko to Dymitr, and her mouth drifts open. Niko thinks of the banshee gaping at Dymitr in Lidia's private lounge, and spares a moment to wonder.

"Wow," she says softly.

"Hello. Hi?" Niko waves a hand in front of her face. "Bloody man here? Can you tell Sha there's a strzygoń here to see her, please?"

Each of the O'Connor-Vasquez hospice care centers employs someone who doesn't feast on human emotion, just to make sure no one is relishing the sorrow *too* much; for this one, it's Sha.

"A—Whoa." She must be young. One of the newest ones. She blinks at Niko, and he drums his fingers on the desk in front of her, drawing attention to his hard, sharp fingernails. She picks up the phone in front of her, and turns away from him as she makes the call.

Ala is starting to look twitchy. She twists the toe of her sneaker into the carpet, which is a mélange of gray, blue, and green. The walls all around them are purple-taupe, and the chairs by the mock fireplace are dusty rose. Sea colors, he thinks, if sea colors were first ingested and then vomited up again later.

Sha strides toward them, her lips quirked in a smile. She's

cut her curly hair into a chin-length bob since he last saw her, and her trousers and blouse are perfectly tailored and pressed, in jewel tones that bring warmth to her skin. There's a deliberate "ordinariness" to her choices that's designed, he thinks, to mitigate just how out of the ordinary she really is.

The hair on his arms stands on end at the sight of her—a typical reaction, he's given to understand. Sha isn't a Vasquez or an O'Connor or even a banshee. She walks on careful feet, with no shadow in her wake, and sometimes when the angle is right, he glimpses a wing over her shoulder, like a coin catching sunlight on a city sidewalk.

Not for the first time, he wonders how the rumor that shedim could turn into *goats* got started. They're the furthest thing from goats he can imagine.

She has a takeout box in hand from the Indian place down the street. As she looks them all over—with equanimity, as if this isn't the strangest thing she's seen tonight—she sticks a fork into her curry and sets it down on the counter, right next to a potted plant.

"Nicky," she says to him. "I thought this place gave you the creeps."

"Don't act surprised," he says. "I know you heard me coming."

She laughs, but doesn't deny it. "I'm allowed the niceties of normalcy, you know."

She tilts her head toward Dymitr, as if straining to hear a whisper, and a small crease appears between her eyes, and Niko wishes he knew what it meant. What she hears about Dymitr's future, minutes or hours from now.

"You're not a banshee," Dymitr says to her quietly.

"Is that a question?"

"No." His gaze shifts to the ground just beside her, where her shadow should have been. He seems to reconsider. "Yes."

"The word you're looking for is sheid," she says.

His next words seem to fall out of him like something tumbling out of a loose pocket. "A demon?"

Niko cringes. Sha gives Dymitr a cold smile.

"*Demon*," she says, "is not our preferred terminology. We eat, sleep, breathe, live, and die just as you do. We simply know more." She tilts her head a little as she acknowledges, "Some of my kind are more . . . *troublesome* than others. But that is true of all of us, including your own people."

Dymitr's cheeks go pink in a way that Niko refuses to find charming. "My apologies. It's not often I encounter . . . someone new."

Niko knows he means *something* new—but he's aware, at least, that he should never call a creature a "something."

"No, you wouldn't have encountered my kind, would you." Her voice is soft. There's nothing menacing about Sha, exactly—but there's something unsettling about a person who knows as much as she does, who hears whispers of what's next. Her quiet is like the sky reflecting on still water: it obscures the depth and the dark of what lies beneath it. "They fled your country during the war along with all the other Jewish people. Or—the fortunate ones did."

People say there are two different worlds, Niko thinks.

Human and not-so-human. But there aren't, really—not when it counts.

Dymitr looks at his shoes, and then back up at Sha.

"I'm sorry," Dymitr says again, and if he had something to add, he swallows it instead.

Sha frowns at him for a moment longer, and then seems to come out of a daze, the crease in her brow disappearing as she focuses her attention on Niko again. "What do you need?"

This is why he loves her—because she really means it. He doesn't explain the situation to her: the flower wilting in Dymitr's pocket, the strzygi who have likely deemed him expendable, the quest to stand before Baba Jaga, the pursuit of the Holy Order. He tells her only that they need a safe haven until sundown, that Ala needs a private room that locks from the outside, per her request, and that he'll owe her a favor—something he doesn't offer lightly, given its rich potential for magic.

"No, you won't," Sha replies, patting his cheek. "You've already paid."

Niko looks away. He doesn't need the reminder—of what he is, and of what it means, and of why it makes her want to be kind to him. So he ignores it.

Sha takes Ala to one of the vacant hospice rooms, where Ala declines a sedative but accepts a clean T-shirt. Ala pulls all the curtains closed, takes off her shoes, and sits on the bed to wait for the curse to hit her. For a moment, Dymitr and Niko stand there, staring at her.

"What are you waiting for?" she says. "Lock me in and leave me alone."

Niko pulls Dymitr out of the room to do as she says.

🦁

Niko nudges the bathroom door open with his toe, and watches Dymitr at the sink. The water is running, and Dymitr's jacket hangs on a hook on the opposite wall, where it would be so easy, so simple to take the fern flower from his pocket and sell it to Lidia Kostka, or whoever wanted to pay the most for it. But Niko doesn't.

Instead, he watches Dymitr peel the blood-soaked handkerchief from his right hand with trembling fingers and examine his exposed nail bed with a grimace. Under the fluorescent lights he looks ghostly. He eases his hand under the stream of water and hisses with pain.

"What are you, a masochist?" Niko says, setting down the first aid kit, bundle of clean clothes, and—thank God—toothbrushes that he scavenged from Sha's supply closets. He closes the bathroom door behind him and reaches around Dymitr to put his hand under the faucet. He creates a kind of shelf with his fingers to slow the flow of water. It dribbles over Dymitr's wounded finger gently.

"Thanks," Dymitr mumbles, and Niko is aware of him, aware of himself. Dymitr's shirt is white cotton, pulled up to his elbows, and there are scars across his knuckles, and he's warm. Niko thinks of him lifting the bow to fire an arrow.

"I brought bandages," he says. "So we can have our Florence Nightingale moment, if you'd like."

Dymitr snorts. "I can handle it, thanks."

"Hmm." He turns off the faucet and takes a paper towel from the dispenser. He doesn't ask for permission, exactly, but he moves slowly enough for Dymitr to pull away as he wraps the paper towel around Dymitr's wounded hand and squeezes, gently, to dry it. Their eyes meet and Niko sees them in the mirror in his periphery, Dymitr an inch or two shorter, their shoulders almost touching, Dymitr's sudden intake of breath. And then Dymitr stepping away.

"You've stopped trying to provoke me," Dymitr says. He flips the toilet seat lid down so he can sit on it. Niko passes him the first aid kit, and then faces the sink himself with a toothbrush in hand. He needs to get the taste of crow blood out of his mouth.

"As a general rule, I don't feel the need to antagonize people," Niko says. "There's plenty of anger in the world already. But it can be interesting to see how people react."

He sticks the toothbrush in his mouth to stop himself from saying more. Dymitr opens the first aid kit on his lap and starts an assembly line of wound-tending: antiseptic, gauze, tape. He binds his third finger and pinkie together, like a splint.

Niko spits pinkish toothpaste into the sink and rinses out his mouth. Then he tugs his shirt over his head and tosses it into the trash can beside him. It's a lost cause.

He can feel Dymitr's eyes on him, but he pretends not to notice. This intimacy is flowing too fast, too much, and if Niko doesn't stop himself, he'll drink it all down at once until there's nothing left.

"Why do your own people fear you?" Dymitr asks, and it's not the first time he's asked, but it's different now. They're alone.

Niko scrubs his hands using the lavender-scented hand soap.

"Male strzygi are rare, and they're sterile," Niko says. "I don't know why that matters, but it seems to. Their sterility makes our leadership feel they're *expendable*." He digs his fingernails into the lines of his hand. "So at any given time, my people designate one strzygoń to serve as zemsta."

"Zemsta," Dymitr says, with more ease than Niko himself says it. "Retribution?"

Niko nods. He stays focused on his task, cleaning the dried blood from his cuticle beds.

"Bound to pursue vengeance against the Holy Order on behalf of all strzygi," Niko explains. "I'd call it a job, but that word implies choice. My predecessor—my cousin Feliks—died a few years ago. Struck down by a Knight, as we all are, eventually. And then the duty fell to me."

"You hunt the Holy Order, only?"

"It's not in my best interest to kill humans, given that they're my food source," Niko says with a sly smile. A testing smile, to see if Dymitr will be alarmed—smiling tends to bring out what's strange about him. But Dymitr meets his eyes without apparent difficulty. "When someone targets innocents among my people, then yes. I hunt them. And I think the world is better for it."

"I'm not inclined to disagree," Dymitr replies. "Is that why Sha said you'd 'already paid'?"

"Yes," Niko says. "Sha feels I've given enough for *creaturekind,* and can expect . . . what does she call it? 'Basic kindness.'" He tries to say it like it's a joke, but it makes his throat ache a little, and it doesn't come out right.

But Dymitr only nods, and says, "How do you know who to pursue?"

"People come to me with names," Niko says. "I investigate. And then . . ." He draws the tip of his thumb across his throat. "I'm better at it than Feliks was. Better than most, I think. And the debt that all strzygi owe me, at all times, means I can always do magic. Which means I will always be more powerful than they are. And that makes them nervous." He shrugs. "Though to be honest, I didn't fit in with them that well before I became their vengeance, either."

"Why not?"

"A story for another time," Niko says. He bends at the waist to splash water on his face, to scrub crow blood out from the corners of his mouth and the underside of his chin. When he straightens, Dymitr is hovering behind him, his hand now bandaged, holding a paper towel.

"If you can always do magic, you could have stopped them before they demanded my fingernail," Dymitr says, a hint of accusation in his voice.

"I could have." Niko suppresses a smile. "But I was interested to see if you would give it. Someone who would do that to help one of us . . ." He shrugs. "Says a lot about you."

Rolling his eyes, Dymitr reaches for Niko—to dab a

smear of blood on the side of his neck with the paper towel he's holding.

"You missed a spot," Dymitr says. "Sorry."

Niko turns and perches on the edge of the sink, looking up at Dymitr. He's standing a little too close, and Niko feels it again, the temptation to take, and take, and take.

"You don't know me," Dymitr says quietly. Apropos of nothing, Niko thinks, except what they aren't saying. "Why are you helping me?"

"I know more than you think," Niko says. Powerless to stop himself, he hooks his fingers through Dymitr's belt loops and tugs him a few inches closer.

"I know you're not afraid," Niko says. "Which is strange, for a mortal, given that I'm actually rather dangerous." He expects this to compel another roll of Dymitr's eyes, but Dymitr receives it with complete solemnity. And perhaps that's fitting. Niko really is dangerous.

He taps Dymitr's sternum with his free hand. "And I know there's a deep well of rage in you. I can feel it, like a prickle down my spine."

Dymitr doesn't contradict him. His gray eyes are intent on Niko's, and his breaths are coming faster.

"Is that why you're helping me?" Dymitr says.

"I'm helping Ala because she deserves it," Niko says. "I'm helping you because you're beautiful."

Niko isn't shy. He never has been. He sees no reason to waste time with his life being as dangerous as it is. If Dymitr finds that off-putting, better to know now, really.

But Dymitr only laughs, as if the idea of him being beautiful is an obvious joke. "Oh really."

"Are there better reasons?" Niko shrugs. "People fight for honor, for love, why not for beauty?"

Niko stands, so their bodies are just barely touching, so his mouth is poised over Dymitr's. He watches Dymitr's Adam's apple bob in a nervous swallow, but still, he doesn't pull away.

"You only know what I've showed you," Dymitr says.

"That . . ." Niko touches his lips to Dymitr's cheek, right beside his mouth. ". . . is true of everyone, all the time."

Dymitr hesitates for just a moment, his warm breaths against Niko's face. He smells like sweat and antiseptic, but it doesn't matter; Niko is still prickling everywhere they aren't quite touching, and warm everywhere they are. Then Dymitr relaxes a little, and turns his face so their lips meet. Despite his initial hesitance, it's a firm, decisive kind of kiss that ends in the hard slide of teeth against Niko's skin. He swallows down a helpless sound.

"I have to go," Dymitr says, his voice rough. Then he's gone, and Niko is alone with the scent of hand soap and chemical cleaner and toothpaste.

7

A DEAL RENEGED

Ala is in the middle of watching a Knight of the Holy Order chop off a czort's head with an ax when Dymitr walks in. It must be afternoon, because she's lucid enough to speak to him, and that wouldn't have been possible earlier.

"Get out," she says, too dully to make an impact.

Dymitr steps right through the Knight standing in triumph over the czort's disembodied head, and sits in the chair next to her bed.

"Would it help if you showed it to me as you watched it?" he says.

She shakes her head. "Not interested in traumatizing both of us."

"I can handle it."

She sighs, but the work of creating illusions is enjoyable to her, the way she imagines other people feel about knitting or cross-stitch. She re-creates the Knight, the czort, the bare country road where they encountered each other beneath a lone streetlight.

"Poor czort," Dymitr says. "I'm given to understand they rarely cause trouble."

"Gentle souls cast as devils in humankind's ongoing stage play of existence. It's Oppression 101: find a bad guy, and if you can't, make one up." The curse has left her sweaty and weak. She wants to go home and wrap herself in her grandfather's quilt and watch television. Instead, she's stuck in this place that stinks to high heaven of dread, one of her least favorite of the fear flavors—like toasted walnut, maybe, or a honey-wheat cracker.

"Will you tell me about the Knight . . ." she says to him, as the vision changes. Now they're in a village square, all cobblestones and stone fountain and hedgerows. The sky is orange-pink from the setting sun—or the rising sun, it's hard to say. She layers the imagery over the hospice room so Dymitr can watch it unfold with her.

Toasted walnut—Dymitr's dread.

"Tell me about the Knight you want Baba Jaga to destroy?" she finishes. The village square is empty, but she's sure the Holy Order will appear soon. They always do.

He asks, "What do you want to know?"

"What did he do to deserve your ire?" She tilts her head. "Or *she*, I suppose. They're letting women do it, these days."

"My ire. Yes, I guess you could call it that."

He clasps his hands in his lap. She notices the gauze around his fingers, the lost fingernail finally bandaged.

In the village square, a black car pulls up to the curb just outside a pharmacy. The neon sign in the window of a nearby bar—a beer logo—is dizzying. It reflects on the tinted car windows.

A woman all in white steps out of the car, her bone sword already in hand.

Ala focuses on Dymitr so she doesn't have to look at that sword.

"There was a girl," he says. "Young. Barely more than a child. She . . ." He smiles a little. "She liked those— turtles. You know the ones? They wear masks in different colors, and fight with weapons—"

"Teenage Mutant Ninja Turtles?" Ala says, with a laugh.

The woman in white is walking toward the fountain. Through the falling water, Ala sees a strzyga woman, with stringy black hair that hangs almost to her waist. The Knight's opponent. Target.

Victim.

"I've been waiting for you," the strzyga woman says to the sword-wielding Knight. So they must be in America, then. The accent is right.

Dymitr nods, his eyes on the illusory scene in front of him.

"Yes. The Teenage Mutant Ninja Turtles. The girl liked to dress as the purple one when she was younger," Dymitr says. "She stole one of her father's neckties and cut eye holes in it. I'm sure he was angry, but he let her keep it. And she used the kitchen broom as a bo staff." His mouth twists a little, like he's trying not to smile anymore, but can't quite help it. "She liked to build things, too. She collected bugs, and leaves, and rocks. And she was a zmora, not yet come into her power, but almost."

Ala feels cold creeping into her. She tries not to watch the strzyga and the Knight circling the fountain, the strzyga in full shift, with the face of a barn owl, the Knight with her sword poised over her palm, ready to summon cursed attackers with her blood.

"And the Knight you want destroyed," Ala says. "He killed the girl?"

"Yes and no." Dymitr looks down. "The girl's mother was afflicted. Schizophrenic, doctors said, though she wasn't convinced—she was zmora, too, and zmora don't typically have conditions like that, as I'm sure you know. But she saw things—heard things. Medication calmed her, but it didn't cure her. She was prone to erratic behavior. One day she wandered off, into town . . . and she attacked a human, an old man. So the Holy Order was called to bring her down. They—the Holy Order usually travel in pairs—went to the girl's house to execute her mother. They generally ignore zmory in favor of more dangerous targets, but once they're informed of one's location, she can't be permitted to live."

He tilts his head.

Ala is frozen. Abruptly, the strzyga and the Knight in white fall away. The village square disintegrates. It's sundown, and the curse has ended its torments for the day, but she can't find it in herself to move.

She knows Dymitr's story—she knows this story already.

Dymitr goes on: "The girl—a teenager by then—begged for her mother to be spared, and when the Knights were unyielding, she tried to fight them off with the kitchen broom. They hurt her enough to subdue her, and killed her mother right in front of her."

Ala listens to the ticking of the clock for a moment as he gathers himself and continues.

"As it turned out, the woman wasn't schizophrenic, but cursed," he says. "When she died, the curse leapt from her body and into the girl's. And the girl grew older afflicted by the same thing as her mother."

Ala's throat tightens. She knows—she knows what he's building toward, but she still can't quite make herself respond.

"When she was maybe eighteen, her father reached out to the Holy Order again. He was human, and he claimed he was unable to contain his zmora daughter any longer. He wanted their help. And they came, a pair of them, and executed the girl, just as they had her mother." Dymitr looks up at her. "The curse leapt down the bloodline to her cousin, who was then living overseas. In Chicago."

Ala.

She looks away, her eyes wet.

"The Knight," Dymitr says, "is one of the Holy Order who was present at both executions. They are taught that humanity is worth. That all the resemblance that a being such as yourself bears to a human is an elaborate trick, a falsehood. It's nothing to them, to kill one of you. Easier than putting down a rabid dog." He spits the words, fierce. She wishes she was like Niko, and could feel his anger, the force of it. She's startled to find a human who feels this on her behalf.

"How did you know Lena?" Ala says softly. Lena, her cousin. Younger than her, but nearer to the curse, which ricochets like a pinball down the bloodline.

"She was a few years behind me in school," Dymitr says stiffly. "After her mother died, I visited her often. Her father was cruel to her. He was afraid of them both, which of course supplied them with ample food, though he hardly ever let them leave the house. After the Knight killed her, I mourned her."

He sits back in his chair. She thinks of the banshees gaping at him at the boxing ring. The receptionist marveling at him when they first walked into this place. It's his grief that draws their attention, Ala thinks. He's full of sorrow, and empty of fear.

"If it were just this Knight's death I wanted, I would have sought out someone like—like Niko, maybe," Dymitr says. "But I want to ask Baba Jaga for something specific. Something more like—unmaking. Something only she can accomplish."

His lower lip trembles, just a little. He's containing it, his grief, but now she sees the little ways it escapes—into the glassiness of his eyes, and the tremble of his fingers, and the flatness of his voice.

"I'm sorry I didn't tell you sooner," he says. "How I know you. I'm sorry for all the things I still haven't told you."

"I don't care about that," Ala says, and she touches his arm, right below the elbow. Squeezes gently. He looks at her, and he looks unbearably vulnerable right now, his gray-brown eyes wide and his hair falling over his fore-head.

"Thank you for helping me," she says.

"Never thank me," he replies, and it's as if her gratitude is so distasteful to him that he can't bear it a moment longer, because he stands and walks out without another word. Ala stares at the chair he just left, puzzled.

He's just told her more about himself than she ever thought he would, but she still feels like she's missing the most important things.

Ala is the last to arrive in the lobby of the hospice center ten minutes later. Niko, standing by the door, wears a T-shirt he got from the lost and found, one with three wolves and a moon on it, and he's not looking at Dymitr. Dymitr, closer to the withering fiddle-leaf fig tree next to the front desk, is shrugging on his jacket, and he's not looking at Niko. Sha, her hair now bound back with black ribbon, is marveling at them both like they're a fire-works display.

"Weird vibes coming from both of you," Ala comments, and she realizes she's just like her mother, unable to bear other people's pretending.

"Contrary to what you've been told, acknowledging it doesn't make it less awkward," Niko says briskly, and he spins his car keys around his finger as he leads the way out of the building.

It's late afternoon, and the air is cool, though the deep

gold of the setting sun hints at summer. Ala used to love the long days of summer, the heat radiating from the sidewalks; the overgrown grass in all the lawns, irrepressible; the clash of bad music from all the bars in Wrigleyville with their doors and windows wide open. The curse took all that from her, making her dread the day, turning winter into a refuge.

"I wish you luck," Sha says to them, nodding to Dymitr and Ala in turn. Niko kisses her cheek, and holds his face there for a moment to say something in her ear. She pats the side of his head, and as she turns, a glimmer—not of light, but of a feather. Ala glances at Sha's shoes, wondering if the rumors of shedim having rooster feet are true. But then, half the rumors about zmory aren't true, either.

"Thank you for your help," Ala forces herself to say, though she's as awkward with gratitude as she is with apologies. And greetings. And introductions.

"Thank Nicky. I did it for him," Sha tosses over her shoulder as she walks back into the hospice center, serene as ever. And then it's just the three of them again.

They find Niko's beat-up Jeep at the far end of the parking lot. Dymitr climbs into the back, where his bow and quiver wait for him. Ala brings the passenger seat back a little too soon, hitting him in the knees.

"Ow!" he says.

"Don't be dramatic," she replies.

His hand darts out and he flicks the tip of her ear. She claps a hand over it, glaring at him. But it was so childish that she can't help but laugh.

"Settle down, children," Niko says, and he starts the engine.

Ala unzips her window as they drive toward the lake, and Niko reaches into the center console to retrieve a CD. She catches a glimpse of it as he slides it into the player: Jimi Hendrix, *Electric Ladyland*. He skips ahead to the fifteenth track, "All Along the Watchtower," and turns up the volume. The wind is picking up as they draw closer to the lake.

Ala is surprised to see Dymitr's lips moving, singing along. Ala lets her hand dangle out of the car, her fingers blown apart by the wind.

Niko is singing, too, his voice harsh and toneless. With a sigh, Ala joins in.

They're on Lake Shore Drive now, and the waves lap up against the rocky shore, against the boats in the marina. The bike paths and parks expand and contract on their right side as they drive, the buildings on their left shrinking down to just a few stories the farther they go. The feats of architecture that make up the city's downtown are just distant giants in the rearview. Niko exits at Lawrence Avenue, and turns down the music.

"My mother took me to meet her once, Baba Jaga," he says as they drive under an awning of trees, their leaves just uncurling. "Uptown Theatre isn't where she lives, but it's somewhere she seems to have a . . . presence. We just have to hope she's curious enough about us to want to meet us."

"The fern flower should help with that," Ala says.

"And the nature of *his* grievance," Niko says, jabbing

his thumb back in Dymitr's direction. Ala notices that he doesn't meet Dymitr's eyes in the mirror.

Niko turns on Broadway, then pulls a wide—and illegal—U-turn to drive down a side street, where he wedges the Jeep between a sagging pickup truck with a rusted bumper and a beige Prius with one tire up on the curb. He leads them to the trunk, where there's a long, heavy wooden box about the size of a tool chest. There's a keyhole in the top—he flips the car key around the key ring to get to the old-fashioned metal one he keeps there, and unlocks the box.

Ala lets out a low whistle, standing on her tiptoes to see over his shoulder. The box contains a variety of weapons, though from the outside it doesn't look large enough for any of them. Swords, mostly, though there are arrows, too, and a few smaller blades. Niko takes out his favorite, a falchion with a gently curved blade and a sharp, tapered point. He rummages in the box for the sheath.

"So what do you do if your car gets stolen?" she says.

"Enchanted box. Bigger inside than it is outside, for one thing. But also, after a while, it would find its way back to me. In London I left it under a hotel bed, and the concierge brought it to me in a daze while I was at a sidewalk cafe. Seemed confused about how he'd gotten there or why."

"Clever," Ala says, as if such a thing were commonplace. Most strzygi—most zmory, too, for that matter—wouldn't be able to perform that kind of magic. Either he had help with it, or the constant supply of magic afforded to him by the duty he bears puts that enchantment within his grasp; she's not sure.

Dymitr runs his fingers over the wood with a wondering look in his eyes. Not as familiar with enchantments, then, Ala thinks. And why would he be? Witches are dangerous enough to deal with when you're a strzygoń; a human wouldn't stand a chance.

"Can I borrow one?" Ala asks.

"Take your pick. I'm not precious about them," Niko says. He glances at Dymitr. "Arrows?"

Dymitr nods. "Please."

When they're all armed and ready, Niko locks the box and leads them back to Broadway, to the entrance of the Uptown Theatre.

The theater has been closed for decades, a former "movie palace" of the '20s that fell into disrepair in the 1980s thanks to a cold day, a burst pipe, and a distinct lack of funds. At least, that was the public-facing story. The not-so-human denizens of Chicago—even young ones, like Ala—know better: the Uptown Theatre belonged to Baba Jaga, and a dispute with another witch, resulting in a particularly unwieldy display of Baba Jaga's destructive power, is what caused the shutdown. The echoes of that magic are still obvious to anyone looking for them; the place radiates power, like it has its own pulse. Even the human pedestrians on the sidewalk out front steer their eyes away from it like they know something's wrong with it, though they obviously don't know what it is.

The facade is grand, an elaborate five-story display of intricately patterned stone, with four pillars standing above the wide marquee that reads UPTOWN. No one passing by seems to notice as they approach the boarded-up double doors. Niko steps just to the right of them and presses his palm to the stone, five fingers spread wide.

A marble sign appears under his palm, set into the stone. He takes his hand away to let the others read it:

If you see, then you know.

If you know, then you don't need to see.

Niko looks back at Dymitr, who puzzles over the words for a moment.

"What you need to know is, there's a door here," Niko says, tapping the marble. "Any guesses as to how you pass through it?"

"I hate riddles," Dymitr says.

"Then you'll hate witches," Niko says.

The part of Ala's brain that she trained with Sunday crossword puzzles flickers to life. *If you know, then you don't need to see.*

"We walk through with our eyes closed," she volunteers.

Niko smiles. "Try it and see."

Ala recognizes the challenge in his voice, and not to be outdone, she steps up to the marble sign, closing her eyes. She steps forward, and the grit of the stone gives way like sand around her body. Passing through the wall isn't easy—for a moment, as she's caught between one place and another, she can't breathe, she feels pressure on every inch of her skin, squeezing her—but then she's standing in the lobby of the theater, gasping.

The first thing she notices is the smell, musty and rotten.

Wet carpet, mold, and broken plaster. But the signs of deterioration are obvious even without her sensitive nose: cracked, peeling drywall on the ceiling, a thick layer of dust over every flat surface, soft materials yielding and buckling with the weight of time as the hard ones stand untouched. The marble floors are intact, though dirty, as are the elaborately decorated walls—pillars on either side of the hall, covered in birds with spread wings and beautiful women in profile; shields and unfurling leaves. At the other end of the lobby are two grand staircases that join beneath three arches. A single chain hanging just above them suggests an old chandelier—gone now, obviously, the chain hanging empty.

The place should be dark. There are no lights that Ala can see, not even emergency floodlights—she suspects that rumors of the theater's restoration are false, fed by Baba Jaga herself so the city doesn't tear down the building—but still the walls seem to emanate a warm light, from everywhere and from nowhere. The effect isn't like lamplight; it doesn't make the space welcoming. It's more like the menace of a distant fire.

They walk under the grand stairs and into the main floor of the theater. The distant stage is wide and shallow in front of the diamond-patterned fabric that covers what used to be a movie screen—she's sure it's not intact anymore. The rows and rows of seats are so dust-covered and chewed apart by pests that it's hard to tell they used to be a deep, rich red. The facades on the walls and ceiling are as elaborate as the ones in the lobby, though a huge white stain, like a salt stain, streaks the left side of the room. The result of the burst pipe—or the scar of old magic. She can tell that in its prime, the theater was a grander, more beautiful place than the Crow. Its deterioration feels like a loss.

The farther she goes into the theater, the stronger the pulse of magic. She feels it pressing against either side of her head like a migraine.

"Is it true what they say about this place, that Baba Jaga destroyed it herself?" Ala says to Niko. "I've heard a few different stories, each one wilder than the last."

Her voice doesn't echo, though it should. She sounds as quiet and flat as she would in an anechoic chamber.

"I think so," Niko says, and at Dymitr's questioning look, he explains: "A witch came to Baba Jaga with a bargain: if she could take something from Baba Jaga without her realizing it was missing, she would receive Baba Jaga's house. But if Baba Jaga did realize it was missing, she could have the witch's magic."

"Her house?" Dymitr asks. "Why would anyone want her house?"

Niko leads them down the left aisle, now out from under the overhang of the mezzanine.

"A witch's home isn't a source of power, exactly . . . more a *container* for it. Take it, and you take a great deal," Niko says. "Baba Jaga, as one of the most powerful witches alive, has a correspondingly more powerful house. It's hard to overstate the audacity of trying to bargain with her for it. It's like an attempt at a coup."

Ala runs a fingertip over the back of one of the seats, and it comes away gray and gritty.

"Baba Jaga allowed the witch to enter this theater, which is a secondary . . . *container,* of sorts . . . to take something, anything. The witch disappeared inside for a few hours, and then emerged, smug and triumphant. Baba Jaga searched her with magic and found that she held only what she'd walked in with—no more and no less. She searched the interior of the theater with magic, too, and everything was in place. It seemed that the witch had taken nothing at all." Niko held up a finger, then turned to point behind him, at the back wall high above them. "But the witch made a tiny mistake. She left a film reel slightly askew, and then Baba Jaga knew—what she took was a matinee showing."

Ala grins. She likes this version of the story. "Nice."

"Not nice enough," Niko says. "Baba Jaga told the witch what she had discovered, and the witch tried to flee before Baba Jaga could take her magic. But you don't renege on a bargain with Baba Jaga."

"What happened to her?" Dymitr asks.

"She was ripped to shreds," Niko says matter-of-factly. He's walking down one of the rows of seats now, toward the wall with its densely patterned facade. There, in the arch of the exit, right by the edge of the stage, is a skull made of stone, set into the wall. Niko traces the outline of the eye socket with his hard fingernail.

"She's buried in the wall here. But Baba Jaga's rage at having been nearly fooled, and by an oath-breaker no less, was explosive. She couldn't contain it. She created a storm inside this place, soaking it through, ripping it apart with wind. Some of it, she restored, but she left the rest, I think as a warning." He shrugs. "Best not to forget what we're up against. Last chance to back out."

"No one's backing out," Ala says.

Niko and Dymitr's eyes meet, and Ala gets that feeling again, that something is strange between them. She smells sweet peach and honey, toasted walnut and warm sage, all intermingled. She can't tell which one of them belongs to which man.

"Please," Dymitr says to Niko.

So Niko draws his blade and presses the meat of his thumb against it, just hard enough to draw blood. Then he touches the bead of blood to the forehead of the skull set into the stone.

"Nazywam się Nikodem Kostka," he says. "Szukam Baby Jagi."

8

A SECRET TOLD

Dymitr's grandmother went with him the first time. Before they set out, they met in the stone chamber to get ready.

The front of Dymitr's family house was redone in a midcentury modern style, as his mother preferred. All primary colors and medium-toned woods and rounded corners. Tables that stacked, chairs that seemed like an italicized version of a regular chair, sofas that stood on skinny legs. The house itself was old, but you'd hardly know it, by the look of the interior.

In the back of the house, though, was the family history. A dim library packed with ancient volumes and nowhere to sit but the rigid seats in the center; a modest chapel with a floor-to-ceiling wooden cross; and the stone chamber, round and sunk under the ground, where the weapons were kept.

His grandmother usually wore soft slacks, long diaphanous skirts, prim blouses with tiny patterns. Today she wore the clothes of a Knight: a vest that Velcroed across her ribs, a leather jacket, duck canvas pants, and boots that laced up to mid-calf. Her hair was in a braid.

"Do you know why your father isn't accompanying

you?" she said. She went to the cabinet at the back of the room and took out a pot of red paint and a brush. Dymitr knew what it was for: a symbol of protection, to be painted over his heart. Most of them didn't bother with it after they had a few kills under their belt, but for those first few times . . . yes.

"No, Babcia."

He unbuttoned his shirt a few buttons, and when she stood in front of him with the open pot of paint, he tugged the fabric to the side to expose the skin over his heart.

"I asked him if I could do it instead," she said. "This will be my last time. I have chosen you to witness it."

She said it as if it was an honor, and it was. Dymitr knew it. He had three siblings, two older and one younger, and yet he was the one she had taught herself, the one she had decided was worthy of her wisdom.

She touched the cold paintbrush to his chest and swept it in a capable circle. She held the brush like a calligrapher held a pen, almost delicate. Almost.

"You have doubts," she said as she drew. "Tell me about them."

He hesitated, and she looked up, sharply.

"Don't pretend," she said. "We cannot rid you of your doubt if you hide it. You must bring it to the light."

She dabbed the paintbrush inside the paint pot, and began filling in the symbol, a six-petaled rosette. It was pagan, as far as Dymitr knew, but if the Holy Order could make use of something, they did—regardless of its origins.

"It's only . . ." He trailed off for a moment as he searched for the right words. "She seemed so human. Getting groceries like that."

His grandmother nodded a few times. She closed the lid of the paint pot, and tucked the paintbrush behind her ear. Then she brought her hand up and smacked him hard across the face.

"Do not trust your eyes more than you trust your duty," she said harshly. "Deception is in their nature; they make you believe that they're close to human, that they're capable of our virtues, but the truth is deeper and darker. The truth is, they are hunger and cruelty personified; the truth is, they can read your heart, and they will prey upon it if you allow them to!"

Dymitr's cheek stung. He blinked the tears from his eyes. The paint was cold on his chest, still drying.

"My dearest boy." His grandmother's voice softened. "I don't intend to hurt you, only to make sure that you remember. Remember what I have taught you."

She touched his cheek, the same one that she had just hit. Her eyes were soft.

"You will be the best of us. You will do things that none of us have managed," she said. "I know it."

For a moment after Niko speaks, nothing happens. Then Dymitr hears something—cracking, and the shiver of dust hitting the ground. The stone falls away from the skull in the wall, leaving the brown of old bone behind. For a moment, Dymitr thinks he can see the face of the witch hovering over it like she's stuck alive in the wall—young, with frizzy yellow hair and a puckered mouth—but then the skull takes its place again.

The eye sockets grow wide, like two tunnels are opening in the wall of the theater, or maybe like Dymitr himself is shrinking; he chokes on panic as his sense of reality warps and bends, and then a massive brown root, as if from the base of the world's largest tree, spills over the edge of one of the eye sockets. It reminds him of the leszy with the daisy growing in his skull, only the root moves with the deadly speed of a snake. It weaves between the theater seats and splits, then splits again, its tendrils spreading down every row like a many-fingered hand. It reaches Dymitr's feet, and he steps around it, but one of the roots snags his ankle and then grows around it as firmly as a manacle.

He looks at Niko, who's drawn the sword at his back and is now hacking at the roots encircling his own ankles, and at Ala, who is hopping from one foot to the other like a child playing hopscotch. Dymitr doesn't bother to take out his bow, he just watches the roots tumble into the space, bulging from the aisles, growing over and around each other until the entire left half of the theater is a labyrinth of bark and old, dusty seats.

Then the roots stop moving, but when Niko hacks at the ones trapping his ankles, they regrow immediately, as if he had never cut them.

"Well, fuck," Ala says, and Dymitr swallows a laugh. He feels like he's teetering at the very edge of his control.

"We're not dead," Niko says, bending down to prod at

the roots that are winding around his legs. "Which means there must be a way to get out of this."

"Could try asking." The only sign of Ala's fear is the quiver in her voice. "Dymitr?"

She wouldn't ask him if she didn't need him to speak Polish, so Dymitr raises his head and says, into the stifling air: "Czego chcesz od nas?"

He feels foolish, speaking to nothing and to no one and expecting a response. But the jaw bone of the skull hinges open, the teeth separating, and a high, inhuman voice speaks.

"What I want," the skull says, *"is that which you are unwilling to give."*

The roots squeeze tighter around his legs, tight enough to hurt.

"Another riddle?" he says, grimacing.

"Hardly qualifies as a riddle," Niko says, smacking a root that's climbed up one of the theater seats and is now reaching for his wrist. "We have to make an offering, each of us. Something we'd rather not offer."

Dymitr bends down to shove his fingers between his calf and the root, to create space. The rough bark bites into his knuckles. "If I have to pull out another goddamn fingernail—"

"Baba Jaga isn't that crude," Niko says. "She'd prefer something more powerful—a secret, or a confession—"

Dymitr yanks his fingers out from under the root so they don't go numb and goes still, his eyes on the floor.

It's not that he doesn't have secrets—it's that he has so

many, so many secrets and so many confessions, that he can't decide which one will do the least damage but still have enough power to satisfy Baba Jaga.

The roots seem displeased with his silence—they squeeze tighter, and grow so they're now twisting around his knees.

"Fucking hell—" Ala grabs the root that's again reaching for her hand and yanks down, breaking it. "Fine. I'll go first. My confession is that I killed my mother."

Dymitr can't help but stare at her, despite the roots creeping around his thighs, binding his legs together. He knows that Niko has killed people—knew the first moment he saw him that he was capable of it. But Ala just doesn't seem like she has it in her.

If Niko is surprised, though, he doesn't show it. He offers his own confession.

"I was not born a strzygoń," he says. "I was changed into one."

For a moment, Dymitr forgets about the roots wrapping around his legs. "That's impossible."

He's never heard of someone *becoming strzygoń* before. He's heard of magic that can store a mortal soul beyond their death, or infusions of magic that empower mortals to perform unnatural feats. He's heard of bites that make ordinary men monstrous, or curses that warp a woman beyond recognition. But rumors of their vampirism are false; strzygi are born, not made.

"Oh, and you suppose that you, an ordinary mortal, understand the limitations of magic?" Niko says, with a quirk of his mouth.

"Dymitr!" Ala snaps. "Now!"

His silence is like a stone rolled over the entrance to a tomb. He's trapped by it, too weak to heave it aside.

"Just *do it*!"

"I am not," Dymitr says, his voice breaking, "an ordinary mortal."

As he speaks it, he's not sure it will be enough. But he knows that as vague as it sounds, the harder they tug on the thread of it, the more of him will unravel. The roots twist away from his knees, release their grip on his calves and ankles. They disappear under the seats behind him. His legs are throbbing, and when he lifts a pant leg to see the damage the roots did, he sees a raw, red welt crisscrossing his ankle.

He's about to ask what the purpose of all that was when he sees, descending from the ceiling like a single snowflake, a scrap of paper. It wafts toward Niko, flutters, and then settles in his outstretched palm, folded neatly down the middle. He opens it.

"It's an address."

"Let's go, then." Ala stalks down the aisle toward the door, and Dymitr follows her, with Niko at his heels.

By the time they step out onto the sidewalk again, it's dark. The night air has never smelled as good to Dymitr as it does then, away from the close, decaying smell of the theater. Petrichor and wet pavement, fried food and cigarettes.

At any other time, it would have been unpleasant, but now, it signals normalcy. Humanity.

They walk to the Jeep together in silence. But when Niko reaches the driver's side door and sticks his key in the lock, he stops, and sighs.

"We could just agree not to talk about any of it," he says.

Ala, standing on the sidewalk by the passenger-side door, kicks at the curb with the toe of her boot.

"I'm not ashamed," she says. She raises her head, and looks up at the Uptown Theatre, where even the back of the building is decorated with patterned stones, diamonds and concentric circles and flourishes. Sections of it are covered with plastic, to keep it from crumbling in the wind.

"My mother was in agony," she says. "She begged me to end it, and I did, even knowing I was furthering the curse along. I thought . . . she had put in enough time. Enough suffering. The irony is . . ." She smiles, and though Dymitr can tell it's forced, it still looks alarming, her inhumanity laid bare. Her cheeks crease around her too-wide mouth, as if straining to keep it contained. "The irony is, it was her suffering that gave me the magic to do it. I put her to sleep, first."

Dymitr braces himself against the back of the Jeep, where the spare tire is fixed just above the bumper. He sees a puddle of rainwater in the middle of the street.

Strange. It hasn't rained in days.

"I don't feel bad about it," Ala says, though she must, or it wouldn't have counted as a confession.

"Good," Niko says. His eyes are like sunlit honey, like the amber that preserves insects forever, like a fire burning low. Dymitr can feel the pressure of his mouth, the tickle of his speech—

"You did her a service," Niko says. "And it took strength."

Ala offers him a small smile. It doesn't reach her eyes.

"And you?" she says to him. "You were . . . born mortal?"

Dymitr has never heard her voice so gentle before.

Niko rolls his eyes. "I had strzygi blood. It was dormant in me. A powerful witch simply . . . awakened it."

"Who?" Ala says. "Why?"

Niko looks at Dymitr as if pleading with him, and Dymitr feels compelled to make his own confession, to finally release himself from the lie that's stood between them from the start of all this less than twenty-four hours ago—

And then an arrow hits the streetlight above them, shattering it so glass rains down on the sidewalk, right next to Ala.

Dymitr has his bow in one hand and an arrow in the other before he draws his next breath. He steps in front of Niko, his back to the car, searching out the source of the arrow. But the moon is hidden behind the clouds, and the streetlight is out, and all the houses along this quiet side street are dark. The glow of Broadway on his left casts long, strange shadows.

He can hear something drawing nearer. Something with heavy, dragging footsteps. No—many somethings, somethings that stoop over the puddle of rainwater to suck it into their mouths, somethings that snort and paw at each other. Pale, hairless things that glow in the faint moon-light.

Upiór. A horde of them.

Most of the quasi-mortal beings of his home country have been called vampires at one point or another. For the upiór, the term is perhaps the closest to being accurate—but they aren't similar to zmory, or strzygi, or even wraiths. In cities they gravitate toward each other, driven by the same need to drink and content to share food sources as long as there's enough to go around. They're creatures of mindless thirst, his grandmother once told him, easy to kill because they're stupid and hard to kill because they keep coming and coming.

And coming.

They're skinny, ungainly creatures, their arms and legs too long for their bodies, their eyes as milky white as their skin. They have long, sharp teeth that stick out from their lips, not lining up quite enough to fit into their mouths. The only sound they make is a loud hissing that reminds Dymitr of a video he saw once of a Madagascar cockroach, recoiling at the jab of a man's finger.

Beside him, Niko shifts, his face morphing into the fierce, inquisitive owl's, his round eyes still the same bright amber. Wings explode from his back, bypassing his cloth-ing by magic, and his trim fingernails grow into claws.

Ala is the first to move. She steps toward the advancing upiór, and she relies on a familiar trick: a dozen copies of her fan out from the toe of her shoe, illusions that seem to confuse the horde. They tumble into each other, confused by the disconnect between their snorting noses and their eyes. Then Ala grabs one and digs her thumbs into its eyes. It's more fragile than a human would be; her fingers pierce its flesh like it's a peach. Dark blood gushes over her fingers and rolls down the backs of her hands. The upiór screeches and lashes out, not at Ala, but at one of the other vampires; the two topple to the street, streaked dark red with blood. They scratch and claw and bite at each other.

Niko and Dymitr move at the same time. With a powerful beat of his wings, Niko rises into the air just enough to stab down at an advancing upiór's chest. Dymitr lets an arrow fly at the one closest to him; it strikes the creature's throat, and it lets out a horrible scream. Dymitr backs up against the Jeep and nocks another arrow and fires again, in one movement. This time he only hits one in the leg, and it keeps coming, clawed hands outstretched.

It's too close now to fire. Dymitr takes an arrow in hand, instead, and stabs at its neck. He hits the juncture of neck and shoulder—not enough to stop it. The upiór's hands close around his throat. Dymitr twists and thrashes, but upiór are strong, and they don't feel pain.

Inspiration strikes, and Dymitr goes limp, letting the creature bear all of his weight at once. Startled, its grip slips, and Dymitr rolls under the Jeep, where its bulk keeps the upiór from following him. Little bits of gravel and glass cling to his palms as he army-crawls beneath the Jeep to get to the other side. He needs more distance if he's going to use his bow and arrow.

He rolls out from under the Jeep, this time on the sidewalk, and then heaves himself onto the hood of the car. In the street, Niko is bringing his blade down on two upiór at once in an elegant, deadly arc; seven versions of Ala lash out with a short sword at once. Only one of them strikes true, but the other six create chaos, turning the vampires against each other in a tangle of pale limbs.

And then Dymitr sees her. Elza. His sister.

She stands at the end of the alley, dressed in black tactical clothing, her hair tied back. Her palms are the color of a port-wine stain, and her eyes glint red. She has a bone sword in each hand, one short and one long. Niko is right in her path, his back to her.

Dymitr told her to go home. Apparently she didn't listen.

"Niko!" Dymitr screams as an upiór's cold fingers tighten around Dymitr's ankle.

The upiór yanks, and Dymitr falls on the windshield, hard. He kicks as hard as he can at the vampire, but its grip is too strong. It clambers up onto the hood of the Jeep, and Dymitr punches it in the jaw, which startles it but doesn't stop it. He twists his free hand behind his back to reach for his quiver, but the angle is wrong, and the upiór opens its mouth wide, its mismatched needle teeth drawing close to Dymitr's throat. Its breath smells like copper and rotting meat.

In the light of the last remaining streetlight, he sees Niko's sword flashing silver as he spars with Elza. Dymitr spits in the upiór's face, twisting his body to break its grip, but he's pinned, he's aching, he's out of options—

Then it screams as Ala grabs it by the head, wrenches it back, and slits its throat. Blood splatters on the pavement. The smell of rot makes him choke.

There's no time to thank her. Elza is only holding one sword now, the other lying forgotten on the street, but she's still besting Niko, quick and deft and deadly. Niko is bleeding from a wound in his side, holding his elbow tight to his ribs. He stumbles, and Dymitr breaks into a sprint.

He loses himself in a rush of adrenaline, grabs his sister's discarded sword, and thrusts it just in time to block her from cutting Niko's throat. For a moment they stand braced against each other right above Niko's Adam's apple, Dymitr's sword pressing up, his sister's sword pressing down. He feels heat in his palms, in his eyes, clawing up his throat like acid.

Now it's *his* palms and fingers that are stained the deep red of the Holy Order.

9

A KNIGHT OF
THE HOLY ORDER

Niko's mortal life was brief, and suffused with the fear of death. Not his own fear—his mother's. She watched his every footstep. He wasn't permitted to do things that other children did, ride bicycles or play in the park or go to summer camp. The only risk that was small enough for Greta Kostka to bear was no risk at all.

But a child determined to find trouble would do so, even within the confines of a house.

She was chopping cucumber, once, so he could dip it in ranch dressing, one of his favorite snacks, when she received a phone call, and abandoned the vegetable on the counter with the knife beside it. Little Nikodem Kostka dragged one of the kitchen chairs over to the counter, turned it, and climbed on top of it so he could see over the counter.

He picked up the knife, which was heavier than he expected, for an object so slim. He took the cucumber in hand, as he had seen his mother do, raised the knife, and brought it down on the vegetable as hard as he could.

The cucumber rolled out of the way of the blade, but his fingers didn't. Blood spurted from his hand, and he screamed so loud Greta dropped the phone and left it dangling from its cord. She seized him around the middle and gathered him to her chest and breathed a healing spell over his fingers, the last of the magic she had left.

Greta sank to the ground with Niko held tightly to her body, so tightly he squirmed, but she didn't release him. He could feel her heart thumping against his cheek, and the tickle of her fast, shallow breaths.

"You can't do this to me, Niko," she said to him, through tears. "You have to be careful. You're so fragile, so fragile. There are so many ways you could die, so many, so many . . ."

She had watched his father die. He was a mortal man she'd met in Jordan, and he had traveled with her for a time; she had not been able to say how long, because time meant little to her. A gentle man, she'd told him, and the kindest mortal she'd ever known. She had loved him, in a way, which was unusual for a strzyga determined only to get a child and return to her family. He went out one morning for coffee and pastries, and he was found dead in the street later that day. Heart failure. It was the suddenness that had rattled her, and now Niko suffered the consequences for his father's mortal frailty.

Niko looked at his hand, still streaked with blood, but healed now. There was a white line across the pads of his fingers, the scar lingering as a reminder.

"I'll fix you," his mother said. "Don't worry, dear; I'll fix you."

She took him to see Baba Jaga a week later. To this day,

he had no idea what his mother traded in exchange for his immortality.

As the Knight's blade comes toward his throat, he thinks there should be something profound about this, that for all his mother's efforts to keep him alive past the tolerances of mortality, his life was cut short anyway.

But that's the lot of every zemsta. The Holy Order are trained from childhood to kill all manner of creatures, and they get the better of every zemsta eventually. The best thing he can do—or so Lidia Kostka told him, when he swore his oath—is take as many of them down with him as possible.

He just didn't think it would happen here, on a quiet side street, with the red light of the Fat Cat Grill sign glowing in the distance, and the smell of french fries on the air.

And then, suddenly: Dymitr is there, his blade the only barrier between Niko and a swift end. His teeth gritted, Dymitr presses the Knight back, at first just a few inches, and then more, stepping between her and Niko. His blade is still crossed with the Knight's. They both hesitate for a moment, and then all at once, they start fighting.

It's only then, as Niko stumbles back and his sowa form—the owl form—recedes, that he sees the purple-red staining Dymitr's hands like a birthmark, and the bright red sheen in his eyes.

Dymitr has an athletic build, and he's capable with a bow and arrow. But nothing Niko saw ever made him think that Dymitr would be like *this*—the blade an extension of him, flashing white as he parries and thrusts and blocks with astonishing grace. Niko has faced a handful of Knights in the last few years, and none of them were like *this*.

Dymitr and the Knight—the *other* Knight—circle each other in the light of the streetlamp. The Knight lunges, sword thrusting at Dymitr's leg; he bats her aside with a twitch of his wrist and slashes at her arm, slicing through the sleeve of her jacket as she turns away from the blow.

His feet are quick as he advances on her, forcing her to trip backward toward the curb. His sword is shorter than hers, but he has reach; he stabs at her, the movement fluid. She blocks him, but he thrusts again, and again, building speed.

They're close to each other now, sharing the same breaths as they strike-block-strike-block, trading blows so fast Niko can't even keep track of them. Then Dymitr swings hard, and the Knight's grip on her sword falters. The bone weapon clatters to the sidewalk, and she trips over the curb behind her, falling hard on her butt.

He holds the sword against her throat, and they both pause.

Her face is streaked with tears. Without the sword in her hand, the red glint to her eyes is gone, and her palms and fingers are back to their usual shade, pale to match her cheek. Seeing them both in profile now, Niko realizes they have to be brother and sister.

The Knight looks a little younger than Dymitr, with

the same light brown hair that appears almost gray, the same stubborn mouth and chin.

"I told you," Dymitr says to her, "to go home, Elza."

He speaks in Polish, which Niko understands, though he sometimes struggles to piece words together himself. In his own language, Dymitr sounds different. His voice is deeper, flatter. Or maybe that's just because he's shed his harmless persona. Maybe this is how Dymitr the Knight speaks.

"You aren't acting like yourself," the knight—Elza, apparently—says. Her eyes flick from Dymitr's to Niko and Ala, in turn. "I thought you could use the help."

Dymitr scowls. "You thought sending a flock of birds to peck me half to death was helping me?"

Ala inches closer to Niko. He knows they should take advantage of Dymitr and his sister's mutual distraction and *run,* but he can't convince his feet to move.

"You were surrounded by strzygi!" Elza replies.

"And now?"

"You got the address you needed," Elza says. "So I sent you a cleanup crew."

She gestures to the pale bodies twisted together on the pavement all around her, the fallen vampire pack.

"You," Dymitr says, as he lowers his blade, "are not helping me. You are an encumbrance. You are a *burden*."

Even Niko can see how the words wound her. He can feel it, too, as if her hurt is the hard press of a hand. He can't feel sadness, but he can feel where rage coils around it like a snake.

"Go home," Dymitr says again, and his voice is cold and cruel. "Or the next time I see you, I will kill you."

He tosses the sword at her feet, and steps back, his eyebrows raised. Elza's tears spill over her cheeks. She grabs the bone sword from the ground, and holds both weapons at once, the handles layered over each other. She bends her head and touches the blades to the back of her neck. Her teeth clack together as she clenches her jaw; the sheathing seems to be as painful as the unsheathing.

We bear the sword, and we bear the pain of the sword— isn't that what they say? Niko has seen this mantra of the Holy Order written, has even heard it from the mouth of a dying man, like a final prayer, not to his God, but to the other half of his soul, buried in that damn weapon.

Elza turns and stumbles into the dark, disappearing between two of the houses on the lonely street and into the night.

Dymitr turns too, slowly, so he's facing Ala and Niko. Up until this point, Niko has felt frozen. But when he meets Dymitr's eyes again, rage prickles through him like blood rushing back into a numb limb. Dymitr's eyes are the color of stone.

Dymitr doesn't have a weapon. His bow and quiver are on the hood of the Jeep, and he gave the bone sword back to Elza. But the thing about facing a Knight is that they always have a weapon—they have the other half of their soul, buried in their spine.

Niko is so on edge, he almost shifts into his owl form right there. He can feel the wings itching at his shoulder blades, the beak scraping at the interior of his nose. To be strzygi is to be twice-souled, the legends say—to have two complete beings inside of you at once. Whichever form he's in, he can feel the other one alive just beneath the surface, waiting to break free. He squeezes the handle of his sword.

But before Niko can so much as twitch, Dymitr grips his gauze-wrapped hand so tightly his knuckles turn white. His face crumples, and he utters words too quiet and too quick for Niko to hear. Then shadow wraps around him, not unlike the black wings of the crows that swarmed them the night before.

By the time it dissipates, he's gone.

"Fuck," Niko says. "Fuck!" He runs his bloody hands over his hair, frantic. "He saw the address, he knows where to go—"

"What is that?" It's the first thing Ala has said since the vampires surrounded them. He can't read her, can only tell that she doesn't feel angry to him, or hurt, or wounded in any way. It's as if the revelation of Dymitr's identity has left her in shock.

She points, and he sees what she's pointing at: a square of brown paper on the street where Dymitr was just standing. Ala picks it up, and cradles it in both hands like it's spun glass. Like it's something precious.

And it is. It's the fern flower.

"He left it," Ala says, frowning. "Why would he do that?"

"He lied to us," Niko says. "I'm not going to marvel at

him having a single shred of honor. Come on, we have to go."

"Go?"

"To Baba Jaga," Niko says. "We have to beat him there. Warn her about what's coming to her doorstep."

Ala seems to register his meaning at last. She nods, the fern flower held against her stomach, and follows him back to the Jeep.

The drive from the Uptown Theatre to the address Baba Jaga sent them via falling piece of paper is only five minutes long. Niko and Ala ride in total silence, all the ease of a few hours ago gone in the wake of Dymitr's confession.

The address takes them to a wedge-shaped building right where Broadway merges with Clarendon. There's a Harold's Chicken at the street level. Fixed above the yellow awnings at the front of the wedge is a billboard advertising a nearby nursing home. A dumpster takes up one of the parking spots on Clarendon.

It's the last place on Earth Niko would expect to find someone as powerful as Baba Jaga, but perhaps that's the point of it. She doesn't want to be found.

Niko finds a parking spot on the street, just a few steps away from the entrance to Baba Jaga's apartment. He unbuckles his seatbelt, but he can't quite get himself to open the car door.

"Maybe he didn't lie to us," Ala says. She's been staring

at the fern flower for the last few minutes, not even looking up as Niko parked the Jeep. "Maybe—"

"He's a Knight of the Holy Order," Niko says hollowly.
"He used us to find the most powerful witch in North
America. His own sister knew what he was doing and
tried to help him. The simplest explanation is that he intends to kill Baba Jaga, or worse."

"I know," Ala says. "Yeah, I know."

They both get out of the Jeep and walk to the door with
Baba Jaga's address marked on it, white number stickers
on the mailbox next to the door. The 3 is a little askew.

He reaches for the buzzer, but before he can touch it,
the intercom above it crackles to life.

"My invitation was for three," a woman's voice says
through the speaker. "Where is the other one?"

"We believe he's on his way here," Niko says. "But we
came to warn you—"

"Silly boy," the woman says. "You think there's something you can tell me that I don't already know?"

The buzzer goes off, and the door's lock clicks. With
a bewildered look at Ala, Niko opens the door, and they
step into the entryway together.

It's all dark wood paneling, glazed over so many times it
looks like it's covered in resin, and black-and-white penny
tile, like every other entryway in Chicago. They climb the
creaky wooden steps to the second floor. The walls are
white, but bulging and cracking where the paint went on
too thick and the heat and humidity wreaked havoc. At the
top of the stairs is a single door with no apartment number

and no name on it. There's a welcome mat, though, that says WITAMY with the Polish eagle behind it.

The door opens without him having to touch it.

The apartment beyond it is big and open, taking up the entire second floor of the humble building. And it's packed with *things,* so many his eyes skip around help-lessly to take it all in. There are dried herbs hanging from the ceiling here and there; a stack of old pots in copper and cast iron and enamel in the corner near a huge hot plate; a cluster of apothecary tables with wicker baskets clumped together on top of them; a stuffed squirrel wear-ing a cowboy hat perched on an old writing desk; a guitar with broken strings hanging on the wall; tapestries de-picting mermaids and dragons serving as rugs; an array of brooms lined up along the wall in the hallway; a green lava lamp in the center of a dining room table, which is also stacked high with old bones.

Standing over one of the tapestries near the windows—which are covered in gauzy green cloth to block the light from the street—is a woman. She's small and lean, with long, straight hair, like a wraith. Her face is shadowed, and she holds a pair of dice in her palm. As Niko steps into the apartment, she lifts her gaze to his and drops the dice at her feet.

"Snake eyes," she says, without looking down. Her voice is low and melodious, pleasant. Just as he remembered it.

She's right, of course. Both dice show a single black dot.

"Back so soon, Nikodem?" she says to Niko.

Niko is too startled to greet her properly. "It's been years."

"Spoken like a born mortal," Baba Jaga says, not unkindly. "So you say you came to warn me. I assume you mean that you've figured out your companion is a Knight of the Holy Order?"

In the green light of the lava lamp, her face is revealed to be young and beautiful. It's artifice, of course; the last time Niko saw her, she looked older, her face lined. But her eyes are the same: unearthly pale, almost colorless.

"You already knew."

"I'm not the oldest and strongest witch in the world for nothing, child," she says.

"We think he might be coming to kill you," Ala says tentatively, and Baba Jaga laughs. As she laughs, she sheds her youth, momentarily appearing as an old woman with a lined face. But once she finishes, the veneer is back in place.

Ala's eyes widen.

"He may have that intention," Baba Jaga says. "But what makes you think it would be that easy?"

"I . . ." Ala closes her mouth, frowning. "I suppose I don't."

"Good answer," Baba Jaga says. She tilts her head, and her eyes lose their focus for a moment. "Ah. Here he is now. Let's ask him about his intentions, shall we?"

10

A TRADE

After the first time, he came home trembling.

It was raining so hard that just the short walk from the driveway to the house washed away most of the blood. But it was still staining his nail beds. He stood in the foyer for a long time alone, staring at them. They didn't seem to belong to him.

Elza found him there. He didn't know how long it had been. There was a puddle of rainwater on the floor at his feet, and he could hear his parents' voices in the kitchen. Elza frowned up at him and wrapped her warm fingers around his wrist.

She led him up the stairs to the second-floor bathroom they all shared as children, before their older siblings moved out and before Babcia moved in. The names "Elza" and "Dymek" were scrawled in crayon under the sink, right above the bottles of cleaning fluid.

She stood at his shoulder and guided his hands into the water. It was warm, which meant it had been running for a while, not that he had noticed. She squeezed soap into her palms and worked it into a lather before rubbing it into his cuticles.

"What happened?" she asked him softly.

He didn't answer.

Elza took out a little brush and used it to scrape the red out from under his fingernails. Then she set it down, turned off the water, and leaned her head into his shoulder.

"It's all right," she said. "You're all right."

"I killed her," he said in a whisper.

"You killed *it*," Elza corrected him. She carded her fingers through his hair, ruffling it. "You did well, Dymek. You did exactly what you're supposed to."

He spared a glance at his own reflection. His cheeks were wet with tears.

You killed it, he tried to tell himself. He tried.

Dymitr can't feel his hands. Or really, he *can* feel them, but they don't seem to be attached to his body correctly; they feel too heavy and too big for him. He squeezes them into fists, briefly, to ground himself, but it doesn't quite work.

Baba Jaga stands across the room, looking no older than he does, but there's something about her that reminds him of his grandmother. Maybe it's the way she reduces him with a single look. Or the way she seems tired of the world and everything in it.

"No Knight has ever come to me before," she says, "and survived."

She moves closer to the table covered with bones, and runs her fingers over them.

Niko and Ala stand to the side, near a waist-high stack of copper pots. Dymitr can't bring himself to look at them. This will be easier if he doesn't.

"Your name?" Baba Jaga says to him.

"Dymitr," he answers brokenly.

"Why?" she asks. "Why that name?"

"I don't know. It's just a name."

Baba Jaga picks up one of the bones—a femur—and holds it like a magic wand, delicate in her fingers. She points it at him.

"It's never just a name, boy," she says. "Dymitr comes from Demeter, Greek goddess of the harvest. A Greek name for a Polish boy. A name of abundant life for a child raised to murder. That . . . is a very special kind of joke. One that only the Holy Order can tell. One that only the Holy Order can laugh at." She wags her finger at him. "My wraith told me to expect you. She told me that you had a strange heart, and that I was in it. Imagine my surprise."

"I can't imagine that very much surprises you," he says unsteadily.

"No," she says, with a hint of that weariness. "Well, enough of this."

She tilts her head.

"Everyone always wants something," she says. "I am not a person to them, I am simply the one who can bring their desires to bear. So tell me. Do you wish to hurt me? To use me for evil?"

"No." Dymitr feels so heavy. So exhausted. His hand

throbs and his shoulders itch. "No, I'm here to ask you to destroy a Knight of the Holy Order."

"You have blood on your hands already," she says. "Why can't you get rid of this person yourself?"

"I . . ." He trails off. He doesn't know where to begin.

"Which Knight?" Ala asks, with a sharpness that suggests she already knows what his answer will be.

Dymitr lets himself go to his knees.

"Me," he says, and he closes his eyes.

"I may not have been honest," Dymitr says. "But I didn't lie."

When he opens his eyes, the room is still bathed in green light from the lava lamp, which is now warm enough for the wax inside to swell into blue bubbles.

He focuses on Ala. She's clutching something to her stomach—a packet of brown paper, faintly glowing from the wilting fern flower inside it. Her wide-set eyes are empty and passive, and he wishes he'd never told her not to lose hope—wishes he'd never done anything to make her like him, no matter how small, because now he's about to crush her.

"I killed your aunt," he says to her. "She was my first mission. I thought, afterward, that something inside me was broken. My siblings both came back from their firsts in triumph, and drank themselves stupid. I tried . . . I tried to act more like I was supposed to, to *feel* more like I was supposed to."

He shakes his head.

"Your cousin—Lena—she troubled me. I recognized her as one of the younger students from my school the moment I entered the house," he says. "And then she fought for her mother in a way that made me doubt what I'd been told. When the curse passed to her, I started to visit her in secret—with her permission. I thought . . . well, I don't know what I thought. And then I found out my sister was assigned to execute her."

He remembers Elza in her jacket, a smear of red paint over her collarbone where their mother had painted the protective symbol. *Where are you headed?* he asked her. *Just some zmora,* she replied, and he knew.

"I tried to help Lena, but I was too late," he said. "I forced myself to admit that every person I'd killed had a soul, just like Lena. And I had to find a way to atone for those deaths." He pauses. Swallows hard. "Those *murders*."

"If you wanted to die," Ala says distantly, "there are easier ways."

"It's not death I want. It's . . . unmaking. Unraveling."

Dymitr looks down at his hands, which are now their usual color. He remembers the stain flowing into them for the first time, right after the ripping of his soul. The heat in his palms and in his eyes, pulsing with his heartbeat, so hot he could barely stand it—

"Knights divide their souls in half—one half resides in our bodies and one half resides in our swords. My request is the destruction of my sword. I'll survive, but I'll be . . . diminished. The world will have one fewer Knight, but I'll

still live to carry the burden of what I've done. It seems . . .
fitting. That I should still have to carry it."

"You've chosen your own punishment." Ala sounds
angry. "You think your victims will be satisfied by your
suffering?"

"I think my victims are dead."

It's too sharp, not quite the tone he intended, but . . .
he meant it.

"I can't be a Knight anymore," he adds, gentler now. "I
have to . . . tear out the part of myself that is."

"You want to wander the earth in pain," Ala says. "But
suffering isn't atonement, Dymitr."

"Then what is?" he asks, and she doesn't answer him. She
looks askance, at first at nothing in particular, and then at
Baba Jaga, who still stands behind the table of bones, a pair
of dice cradled in her palm. Dymitr almost forgot she was
there.

"You can't allow this," Ala says to her.

"It's his choice, not yours," the witch replies. "I suppose
that before I *unmake* you, boy, you have a suggested use
for that special item she's holding? It bears your fingerprints, not hers."

"She's afflicted by a bloodline curse," Dymitr says. "I
thought if anyone could break it, it would be you. With
the fern flower."

Baba Jaga raises her eyebrow at Ala. Ala holds out the
packet of paper, and unwraps it, revealing the red flower
within, emanating light like a firefly. It looks limp, but its
color hasn't changed since he first picked it.

The witch nods.

"I see," she says. "They were right to name you for the harvest, weren't they?"

Baba Jaga leans over the fern flower, her hair draping over Ala's hand like a curtain. Ala is afraid—afraid that the witch will straighten and declare that the fern flower is defective, or too old now to be useful, or not a fern flower at all, the process of picking it an elaborate ruse to trick foolish mortals. She isn't sure she can bear it. She's been feeling the curse creeping through her, devouring her eternity, for the last several years, without understanding. It was like watching water go down a drain. She wasn't human, with a human's limited awareness of mortality. She was supposed to last, and trimming her centuries down to a handful of years was a cruelty she was hardly able to endure.

But now she can have them back. If only Baba Jaga chooses to give them to her.

Ala glances at Dymitr. She can hardly look at him now, knowing what he's done, what he is, what he intends. But he meets her eyes for only a moment.

Baba Jaga straightens, a smile playing over her lips. One of her incisors—pointier than the norm—sticks out like a fang for just a moment before she tucks it away again.

"Very well," Baba Jaga says. "The fern flower's power lies in its ability to attract and devour dark energy. Mortals have misinterpreted this, as they so often do, to mean that it will bring them wealth or luck or good fortune, but really it is like a poultice that draws pus from an abscess; it is useful only if you are already afflicted. Take it into your body, and it will draw the curse away from you. But the paradox of it, for you, is that since you aren't mortal, you cannot touch it without dying. But you will die without touching it."

Ala waits, expecting more—a recipe, maybe, or a set of instructions, like crushing the flower beneath a full moon and circling a fire three times, something an ancient and powerful witch might say. But Baba Jaga only gazes at the flower still held in Ala's hand with a glint of greed in her eyes.

"Then what do I do?" Ala says.

"How did you pick something you weren't allowed to touch?" Baba Jaga says. "How did you carry it without being able to bear it? Yet you ask me how you can take it in?"

"Witches and their riddles," Niko says, sounding almost bored. But the light in his eyes reveals that he's anything but.

Dymitr considers the flower, his head tilting. He's still on his knees, his hands limp in his lap.

"*I* did it for you," he says, after a moment of thought. "*I* picked it, *I* bore it." He glances at Baba Jaga. "So I can swallow it for you, too."

"I don't understand," Ala says. "How can it work as a . . . poultice, if it never enters my body?"

"You have spent too much time with mortals if you expect magic to move in a straight line," Baba Jaga replies.

She points at Ala, and then bends her index finger so it's shaped like a hook. "Magic is crooked, and so are we."

She turns to Dymitr.

"I will transfer the curse from her to you," she says. "Then you will eat the petal, and it will be gone. But it will only work if you are willing to take it in."

Dymitr's gray, solemn eyes are on Ala's.

She knows she should hate him. He's an enemy of her people—of all who walk the earth who aren't human. He killed her aunt and failed to save her cousin. He was the reason the curse ever leapt to her in the first place. And he lied to her, to Niko. Manipulated her.

But all she can think about is how young he must have been when he was sent to her aunt's house to kill a zmora— barely more than a child. She remembers the look in his eyes in the back of the car when he told her not to lose hope. How soft his voice was when he promised he wasn't toying with her.

"Of course I'm willing," he says to Baba Jaga, to Ala.

Baba Jaga beckons them into the next room—so to speak. All the rooms of Baba Jaga's house appear to be part of a continuous whole. But the walls narrow at one point, and Dymitr tugs a curtain back from a window to see, not the glow of the Harold's Chicken sign below them, but the winking lights of the Chicago skyline and the shimmer of the river in the moonlight. He stares, forgetting to be subtle about his snooping.

"Crooked," Baba Jaga says to him, and she brushes a fingertip down his arm. The shadow of a nearby bookcase falls across her face, and Dymitr sees deep lines around her mouth that weren't there before, reminding him that she's far older than she appears. He shivers, and pulls away from the window.

The apartment is indeed crooked, far larger inside than it should be, in addition to—apparently—being in the wrong building. After the walls narrow, they open up again, and Dymitr's ears pop, as if he's suddenly changed elevation. There are no windows in this part of the apartment, only a heavy wooden table that looks older than the city itself, with herbs hanging above it in dry bunches and ribbons dangling among them in every color. A huge mortar and pestle made of stone stand in the center of the table, dusted with whatever she was grinding up last. Jars of shriveled and dry ingredients are in dense clusters at the edges of the table and on narrow shelves fixed at random heights to the walls behind it. He thinks he sees eyes staring at him from one of them, and there's another one full of dark liquid that looks like blood.

He doesn't know how she intends to transfer a dark curse from Ala to him. But when she takes a paring knife from her pocket, and plucks a red ribbon from the ceiling with a flourish, he doesn't flinch.

"Your hand," she says to him, and he gives it to her, resting his knuckles against her palm. She digs the paring knife into the meaty part of his thumb, suddenly and fiercely enough to make him wince. Blood bubbles up from the wound, and he ignores the stinging in his palm to watch Baba Jaga gesture for Ala's hand, too.

Ala holds it out to her. Baba Jaga seizes it and cuts it without ceremony. Holding Ala's wrist, she turns the zmora's hand and brings it down on top of Dymitr's, so their blood intermingles between their palms. Ala looks up at him, startled, as Baba Jaga ties the red ribbon around their hands. She whispers words he can't hear over them.

Ala's fingers lace with his. She doesn't really look like Lena, and doesn't sound like her, either. They grew up across the world from each other, in different generations, speaking different languages. But Lena spoke of her fondly, Aleksja, her last remaining cousin, the American, gentle enough in spirit to live among mortals but fierce enough to endure their cruelty.

Baba Jaga knots the ribbon, and steps back. Somewhere in the apartment he hears the ticking of a clock. Then pain, deeper than the shallow cut in his palm, reaching its white-hot fingers all the way down his arm. His knees threaten to buckle; he locks them, tightening his hold on Ala.

Blood spills from between their palms, first just a trickle and then a flood of it, splattering over Baba Jaga's worn carpet. It's darker than it should be, almost black, and the purple-red stain of the Holy Order creeps over his fingers; he can feel the heat of it in his eyes, the Knight in him emerging.

Then he's opening the door to his grandmother's room on the first floor of his father's house. His hand, pressed to the lacquered wood, looks softer than he's used to, the fingertips not yet callused by a bowstring, the knuckles not yet marked by scars. He looks over his shoulder to see Ala standing in the hallway behind him, looking startled, and he tries to speak to her, to explain, but he's powerless to make a sound.

The room beyond smells like faded perfume. He's been in there only a handful of times in his life, mostly to fetch things for his elders. He's never been welcome to explore it, which was a hardship for the curious boy he was, because it's full of objects. There's a line of medals on the bureau, from wars he wasn't alive to witness; stacks of photographs on the bookshelves, in front of old volumes with gold lettering; glass figurines on the bedside table; journals piled on the foot of the bed; coins from every country in little glass dishes on the desk. So many things to touch and turn over and look through, and he's never dared.

His grandmother—Joanna is the name she chose when she became a Knight, so it's the only name for her he's ever known, selected to honor Joanna D'Arc—sits in a chair by the window. Beyond it is the gate, and beyond that, the street. A lantern burns on a little table in front of her. She prefers its light to an electric lamp. Knights are long-lived—not quite as long as the creatures they hunt, but longer than a typical human life—so he's not sure how old she is, exactly, but when she was born, electricity wasn't abundant. She told him once that she never got used to it.

Her face is lined, the skin of her hands as fragile as paper, the veins showing beneath it. But her back is still straight, thanks to the bone sword buried in it. She's still strong.

"Boy," she says to him. "Come."

He crosses the room, and goes to one knee in front of her, a soldier presenting himself to his commander.

"Babcia," he calls her. "You asked for me?"

"I did." She sits forward, her hands folded over her lap, and studies his face. Her teeth are crooked.

"Your ceremony is in the morning," she says. "Are you prepared?"

"Yes, Babcia."

"Are you afraid?"

He blinks at her, startled. No one has ever asked him that before. He assumed it didn't matter whether he was afraid or not.

"Yes, Babcia," he says, because he is. He's so afraid he hasn't slept through the night in months. There are so many reasons he's afraid. He isn't sure that he can kill. He doesn't like pain. He doesn't want to split his soul in half.

The old woman nods. "I can see it in you."

She doesn't reassure him, and he doesn't expect her to. No adult in his life has ever reassured him, not about the dark, or about the monsters that lurk in it, or about the violence of the world beyond their walls.

"But you will do your duty," she supplies.

"Yes, Babcia."

"Good." She sits back, and picks up the journal, bound in blue leather, that rests on the little table near her. "I have summoned you here to give you a secret. Each of my living descendants is entrusted with one on the eve of their ceremony, so that the knowledge of this family is preserved from generation to generation, yet no one person must bear the weight of all that I know. When you are my age, you will have as many secrets as I do, and you will bestow them on your children and your children's children in just this way. Understand?"

He doesn't, but he nods anyway.

She offers him the journal, and he takes it in both hands, as if it's something precious.

"This is a book of curses," she says.

"Curses? Like a witch's curses?"

"No," she snaps. "Not like a witch's curses. These are the curses of a Knight."

He raises his eyebrows.

"Some of our number know how to forge our weapons; some keep the grimoires of knowledge about our enemies; some keep the texts of our names and histories throughout the ages; *you* will keep our curses." Her eyes glitter. "Our magic."

"I . . . didn't know we could do magic, Babcia," he says to her, feeling uneasy. "Isn't that what monsters do?"

"Did you think the splitting of the soul was not done through magic, boy?" She shakes her head, and a strand of white hair escapes her braid. She tucks it behind her ear with clumsy fingers. "Our magic is not like their magic. It is not offered in repayment of debts; it is costly, righteous, and bloody. It is one of our most important weapons in fighting back the forces of darkness that threaten to claim our world."

He stares down at the journal in his hands. It suddenly feels too heavy to hold.

"Listen," she says, and he so rarely receives this kind of focus from his elders that he can't look away from her. "We are long-lived, and we are strong. But we do not have the same innate power as the monsters we fight. With this book, I can not only summon stronger weapons to fight my enemies—I can make those fights unnecessary. I can turn *their* powers against them; I can create wounds that do not heal; and I can even, on occasion, attach a curse to their blood that will wipe out their entire family line. All I need to give . . ." She runs a finger along the outside of her forearm, where he can see the dark line of a scar. ". . . is a little pain."

He's heard of his mother summoning crows, his father summoning wolves, of a trail of blood that can bewitch a single sigbin or an entire pack of upiór, of pain that lights fires and rends flesh and muffles screams. But he's never heard of the kind of magic that warps a creature's powers or creeps through their blood. He wonders how many times she's used it; he wonders what, exactly, she's done.

"Our task as Knights is to step closer to the dark so that other humans, humans less suited to bear its influence, don't have to. And these curses . . . these curses are even closer to the dark than most Knights dare to go," she says. "None of my children had the disposition for it, so I withheld it from them. But I believe you can bear this burden, Dymitr. You can be our curse-bearer."

She lays a cold, dry hand against his cheek.

"Before you sleep, you must do penance for your fear," she says. "Ten times, to root it out from your heart before your ceremony tomorrow. Understand?"

He suppresses a shudder.

"Yes, Babcia," he says, clutching the book to his stomach.

A PROMISE KEPT

When he surfaces from the memory, he's on his knees in the dark blood he and Ala spilled on the carpet, his hand still clutched in Ala's with the ribbon binding them together. She looks at him with an expression he can't name. She lifts her free hand like she's going to touch his face, and then she doesn't—she lets it drop back into her lap instead.

"The petal," she says to him.

She reaches into her pocket for the brown paper, and offers it to him. He unwraps it as carefully as he can, given how hard he's trembling. The fern flower rests inside it, almost as fresh now as the day he picked it, which feels like it happened in another life. It looks almost like a lily, with big, thick petals that taper to an elegant point, symmetrically arranged around a central labellum. He pinches one of the petals and breaks it away from the flower. It doesn't feel like it's as powerful as it is, but maybe that's just how powerful things are—like the zmory, like Baba Jaga herself, they don't always need to declare themselves.

He puts the petal in his mouth, and chews it. It tastes like *green,* there's no better word for it—like grass, or leaves, with just a hint of sweetness. He swallows, and as he swallows he can feel the petal carving a line of heat down his esophagus and into his stomach.

Pain comes again, but this time it's less focused, and more of a burning that envelops his entire body at once, as if he's been thrust into a fire. Heat swallows him up, and he can tell by Ala's whimper, across from him, that she suffers the same thing; they reach for each other at the same time with their free hands, and clutch each other, the ribbon straining around their knuckles.

Their eyes meet, and the pain disappears. He sits back on his heels, panting, the fern flower fallen to the carpet by his ankle.

Baba Jaga bends over them and cuts the ribbon with the paring knife. But they don't release each other right away.

"It was her," she says to him in a whisper, like it's a secret.

"It was," he says. "And she chose me as her successor."

He says it bitterly, because he knows what it means: that she saw in him the same capacity that she feels in herself. He peels his fingers away from her hand. They're tacky with blood.

"But you aren't," she says to him. "You came to me instead."

But he can't look at her, can't possibly bear her mercy now.

The smell of this place is familiar to Niko. All witch houses seem to smell the same, like lavender and smoke and salt. And now blood, of course, the combined blood of Ala and Dymitr staining the rug between their knees. As they pull their hands apart, Niko is relieved to see their bleeding has slowed, the wounds returned to normal. They come to their feet, and Niko bends to pick up the ribbon that fell between them. He knows Baba Jaga too well to leave her with such a token; there's a lot she could do with it.

He tucks the ribbon in his pocket. He wouldn't have said, before, that you could see the curse on Ala . . . but he can certainly see its absence. She stands straighter, and her eyes are brighter. He doesn't know much about the visions that haunted her, except—*It was her,* she just said to Dymitr, and he seemed to understand. Something strange has passed between them, something Niko can't comprehend.

Baba Jaga is waiting. Niko can tell by the restless shift of her bare feet. Her toes are red with Ala's and Dymitr's blood. Her eyes lift to meet his, and for a moment he sees a spark of light there, like a child's delight. It's a feat for a woman who has seen and done so much, to still find room for wonder.

"And now we come to the main event, I think," Baba Jaga says, when Dymitr turns to face her, Ala and Niko at his back. She leans against the table behind her, jostling some of the jars with the heels of her hands. Teeth clatter together in one of them; live moths flap their wings against the glass in another.

"Make your request, Knight," Baba Jaga says to Dymitr.

"I'd like you to destroy my sword," he says to her. "So the powers and the oaths of my kind are beyond my reach."

"You wish to hobble yourself," Baba Jaga says. She tilts her head a little as she regards him, and it's easy to see the strzyga buried deep in her blood, this way. Baba Jaga is neither strzyga nor zmora nor mortal nor wraith, yet she's collected bits and pieces of so many things in her long years that she can, at times, resemble every one of them.

"Why?" she asks him.

"I have done wrong," Dymitr says, and he sounds exhausted, just as he did in the foyer.

"And you were taught that pain is penance," Baba Jaga says.

Dymitr receives this in silence. Niko looks at Ala, who is biting down on her lip almost hard enough to draw blood. The look she gives him carries a question. He suspects it's something like, *Are we really going to let him do this?* And if Niko didn't believe so much in letting people make their own choices, perhaps the answer would be no. But he does.

Doesn't he?

"Very well," Baba Jaga says. "I have heard that the longer you go without drawing that blade, the more difficult it is to unsheathe. Is that true?"

Dymitr nods.

"How long has it been?"

"Over a year."

"Then I suggest you kneel."

Dymitr looks at his hands, and Niko looks with him.

His right pinkie is taped to the finger beside it and wrapped in gauze—the fingernail he gave to Lidia. His palm is cut from taking Ala's curse. His fingertips are bright red, irritated from the bowstring.

Dymitr takes off his jacket and tugs his shirt over his head. Niko swallows a gasp.

He can see the sword buried in Dymitr's spine. It's a longsword, the hilt flat against his shoulders, but so deeply submerged in his flesh that Niko can only see a sliver of it where it catches the light. He knows from experience that the blade itself is bone white, but he can't see it; it's inside Dymitr's body, and he'll need to pull it free with his bare hands.

He holds the jacket and shirt out to Ala, and she takes them, her eyes wide. Dymitr glances at Niko.

"Might not want to watch," he says to Niko and Ala.

"If you have to feel it, the least I can do is see it," Niko replies, sharp.

Dymitr turns away, and kneels at Baba Jaga's feet. He draws a deep, slow breath, then brings his hands up to the back of his neck. For a moment they hover there, trembling.

"Dzierżymy miecz," he says softly, "i znosimy jego ból."
We bear the sword, and we bear the pain of the sword.

Then he digs into his own flesh. A shudder travels through Niko's entire body. Beside him, Ala presses a palm to her mouth, as if to stifle a scream. Blood spills down Dymitr's back, around his fingertips. He digs still deeper, harder, and makes a strangled sound, something between a whimper and a scream.

Niko steadies himself. Everything in him wants to launch himself at Dymitr and pull his hands away from his back—to save him from this unnecessary agony. But he won't, and it's too late now, besides.

Dymitr screams into his teeth, and plunges his hands into his flesh to wrap them fully around the hilt, which is lifting away from his spine now, soaked in blood and skin and muscle. Dymitr sags over his knees with a sob, but the job is not done; the blade is still buried inside him.

For a moment Niko thinks he's given up, that he won't be able to finish. But then Dymitr sucks in a sharp breath, and straightens, and screams again as he yanks the sword upward. It pulls free of the sheath that is his spine, and he holds it aloft for a moment, blood soaking the blade, the hilt, his hands and forearms.

The open wound in his back is already knitting together, the skin sealing where he broke it with his fingernails. He drops the sword at Baba Jaga's feet with a clatter, and falls forward onto his hands and knees, gasping. Niko's knees feel weak with relief. Ala closes her eyes.

Baba Jaga bends down to examine the sword. She seems unmoved by the display of pain she just witnessed; her eyes glint as she looks over the blade, the simple gold-plated hilt. The instrument of so many nightmares: the bone sword of a Knight of the Holy Order.

"Are you certain?" she says to Dymitr.

Dymitr lifts his head. He hesitates for just a moment, and that moment is all Niko needs.

"Wait!" he says, the word tearing its way out of him. Baba Jaga raises an eyebrow at him. He falls to his knees beside Dymitr, laying a hand on his bare and bloody arm and turning him to face Niko.

Niko's hands are cold against Dymitr's shoulders.

"Don't do this," Niko says to him.

"Do you know how many of your kind I've killed?" Dymitr says to him, his voice rough.

"No, but—"

"Neither do I," Dymitr whispers. "I didn't keep track. It didn't occur to me that the number would matter. Don't you understand? I have to do something; I have to."

"Pain is not penance." It's Ala who speaks this time. She draws Dymitr's eyes up, over Niko's shoulder. "You hurt me, you killed people I love, but I still have no use for your pain; I still don't want you to destroy yourself."

"It's not just that," Dymitr says. His hands come up to Niko's elbows, unbearably gentle. His gray-brown eyes are soft. "I can't *be this* anymore. I can't bear it."

"Then be something else instead," Niko says firmly. He looks up at Baba Jaga. "Change him."

"You say that as if it's simple," she says.

"You changed me into a strzygoń," he says. He doesn't mean to say it. His connection to Baba Jaga is private. But then, these two already know more than anyone else does about him—when his mother died, the secret of his mortal origins, the other secrets he carries, they died with her, and he has kept them alone since then. It's something of a relief, to share that burden.

Baba Jaga seems unfazed by his disclosure.

"You already had strzygi blood," she says with a shrug. "I merely amplified it."

Niko looks down at Dymitr's hands, at the wound in his palm. He thinks of the ribbon in his pocket, stained with Ala and Dymitr's intermingled blood.

"He already has Ala's blood in him," he says. "Zmora blood."

Baba Jaga brings a finger up to tap against her lips, considering the wound just as Niko did.

"Interesting," she says.

She pulls away from the desk, and walks on silent feet to one of the windows, pulling back the curtain to look out at the city. Niko has walked through this apartment before with all the curtains drawn; he knows its impossibilities, how it stands on the edge of the Chicago River in the Loop, but also on top of the Harold's Chicken in Buena Park, but *also* overlooking Hyde Park, depending on which segment of the apartment you're in. Still, he finds himself amazed by the line of light along the river. Chicago always reminds him of a stray line from T. S. Eliot—*Unreal City, under the brown fog of a winter dawn*—though he knows, of course, that the line refers to London.

Baba Jaga lets the curtain fall back across the window, and turns to Dymitr, Niko, and Ala again.

"The payment I require for changing you," she says, "is your sword."

Dymitr stiffens beneath Niko's hands.

"My soul, you mean," he says.

"A piece of it. Yes."

"And what will you do," Dymitr says quietly, "with a piece of my soul?"

"What I wish," Baba Jaga says.

The back of Niko's neck prickles. His mother was in Baba Jaga's debt, once. She refused to tell him what the witch asked of her, but he saw its aftermath. Night after night, for a year, his mother came home with dirt caked under her fingernails and sweat curling her hair and trouble in her eyes. It's no small thing, to be the hands and feet of Baba Jaga.

"Will you ever return it to me?" Dymitr says.

"For the right price," she replies.

There's that, at least. It's a door left cracked, instead of closed and locked. Dymitr looks at Niko, and then Ala.

"Is this what you want from me?" he says. "To change?"

She crouches in front of him, and reaches for his hand. He gives it to her, and holds on.

"I want you to live," she says. "I want you to try."

It takes a long time, but finally, Dymitr nods.

12

A MONSTER'S DEATH

When he told his grandmother he wanted to go to America to find and destroy Baba Jaga, she considered him for a long time.

They were at the coffee shop where she'd once picked out a zmora from a crowd of strangers. He drank his coffee black, now, with honey instead of sugar. He bit down on the hard biscuit that came with it, and met his grandmother's gaze.

"Why?" she asked him.

"Why keep fighting foot soldiers when we can take out a general?" he said. "You told me, once, that you believed I would do things that none of our people have managed. Do you still believe that?"

His grandmother sipped from her cup of coffee. He could see the stiffness in her shoulders that came from leaving the bone weapon sheathed. She was too old to draw it now, her long life finally coming to its close. But her mind was sharp as ever, and for a moment, he was afraid that she would see right through him.

"Perhaps I do," she said, with a small smile.

Baba Jaga picks up a jar of teeth and tips one into her palm, then grinds it to dust in the huge mortar she keeps on the table. She's stronger than she looks, her bicep bulging in her sleeve as she presses down with the pestle.

"Niko, dear," she says, without looking up. "Be a good boy and fetch me a dried thistle."

Niko moves around the table to search the shelves behind Baba Jaga, and Dymitr frowns. He'd gotten the impression, before they arrived here, that Niko had only met Baba Jaga once before. She was the one who turned him from mortal to strzygoń, but he seems to know this place with more than a passing familiarity.

Babcia, he called her, when they arrived.

Niko plucks a jar from one of the shelves and takes a dried thistle from within it with two fingers. He offers it to Baba Jaga, who adds it to the powdered tooth in the mortar and grinds it up.

Dymitr picks up the bone sword that he unsheathed from his body. It hums with the same feeling of rightness a person gets in their sleep when they shift into a comfortable position. He wonders if that will change, when he transforms. Will this piece of his soul ever feel like *his* again?

He expected to feel relief when he came to this decision not to live a half-life, to spare himself the pain of his unmaking. Even a Knight plagued by guilt is a human being, driven by the desire to spare himself annihilation, isn't he? But he feels regret instead. He knows how to bear pain, has been diligently instructed in the art of it since he was a child. Penance, before he took his oaths, and the splitting of his soul that accompanied them, and the unsheathing of the sword that came after, they were all ordinary to him. It would be easier, in some ways, to bear the pain of the sword's destruction, than to embrace whatever *this* is.

Ala's eyes find his.

"Foolish hope, remember?" she says to him, and some of his regret ebbs away.

Baba Jaga pours the mixture into a pot, and sets it on a hot plate to boil. Her fingertips are stained green.

"I can't say what you'll become, exactly," she says. "No ordinary zmora, to be sure. Magic is not mastered and it moves as it will, even through me. But the allegiance you feel to the Holy Order will be broken. They will hunt you as if you are a dangerous animal, and that is, I assume, what you want. To make an enemy of those to whom you once belonged."

He wouldn't have put it that way, maybe, but she's right. He began the process much earlier than this, too. When he fought his sister with her own sword, defending Niko's life with his own. When he fled the Holy Order with a series of grand lies in his wake, and came to this city with only his bow and arrows and a bag of necessities. And even before that, when he refused to draw his sword at all for months, and honed his skill with the bow instead, so he wouldn't have to touch the hilt that weighed heavy on his shoulders. He has been betraying them since before Lena died. At least now he'll do it thoroughly.

Baba Jaga takes the bubbling mixture from the hot plate and pours it into a mug. It's dark red in color, and thick as syrup. She offers it to him, and he takes it in both hands.

"Drink it all," she says. "Then you'll fall asleep, and when you wake, the world will have one fewer Knight."

He holds the mug against his sternum. Despite the fact that it was just simmering on the hot plate, it feels like ice against his chest. Then he raises it to his lips, resolved to swallow it all at once. The last things he sees are Niko's fire-bright eyes and Ala's freckled nose.

He turns his face into the worn yellow pillowcase and takes a deep breath. It smells like detergent—the starchy, industrial kind they use for hospitals. He takes a deeper breath, and he can smell something else, too. Bacon. Lavender. And something sweet as powdered sugar.

He opens his eyes, and finds himself staring at Ala.

She's sitting in a chair beside the bed. She looks different than she did when he last saw her. It takes him a few seconds to realize it's that she no longer looks even faintly monstrous to him. She just looks like Ala: half stern, half soft, always skeptical, rarely unsure.

"Hello," she says to him.

"Something smells sweet," he replies. He turns his face into the pillowcase and breathes in, but he can't find the scent there. She laughs a little, and holds her hand out to him so he can smell her fingers, like a dog.

But then he smells it, that powdered-sugar scent. Pleasant, and light, like angel food cake.

"I'm worried about you," she says. "That's what it smells like."

"Makes me hungry," he says. "That's *annoying*."

"You'll get used to it."

Dymitr considers her. She never struck him as a tenderhearted person before. Yet here she is, sitting in an uncomfortable chair next to his bed, fretting over him.

"You're worried about me?" he says. "Why?"

"You just haven't thought about it," she says. "You were made from the same blood as me. That means you're my brother, and I'm your sister, and we'll always worry about each other from now on."

"Brother and sister." He thinks of Elza, with a sharp pain, and rolls onto his back to stare at the ceiling. There's a crack there, where the paint has bubbled away from the drywall. It reminds him of the lines in his palm.

He looks at her again.

"Are you sure you want a brother who's done what I've done?" he says.

"You'll find there's a lot of family drama among zmory," she says, with a smile that he thinks would have looked menacing to him before, but now seems gentle. "We wouldn't be the first to reconcile after one has killed another's aunt."

"Really."

"Really," she says. "Eternity is long, Dymitr. Time enough for hearts to soften."

He wonders what he would look like to a llorona now.

If the halo of sorrow around his head would still be as brilliant to them, or if untangling the curse from Ala's blood, and hearing that she wanted him to be whole, has healed over some of the loss that divides him.

He sits up, and he startles himself with how quick the movement is, and how forceful—he falls to his knees on the carpet right in front of the bed. Ala laughs.

"The old legends used to say that we could transform into a hair and fit through a keyhole," she says. "We can't, of course, but we do tend to be fast and light."

He lifts a hand and stares at it. His fingernail has grown back, and the wound in his palm is healed over. He comes to his feet, and meets his own eyes in the mirror above Ala's dresser.

He looks like himself—there's some relief in that. His eyes are still that odd shade of brown-gray, his hair still matches them, as before. The scar in his lip is still there. But there is something different about him, too. Something sharper, and wilder, like a fox that wanders into a suburban neighborhood in search of food—capable at any moment of ferocity.

Ala stands beside him, and he sees some similarity between them. That keenness.

"Sister," he says to her, and she nods.

"No visions?" he asks her. "Memories?"

"Gone," she replies, and she smiles so wide it looks like it might split her face in half. "Let's go say hello to Niko. You can find out how worried *he* is."

She leads him out of the room. The scents of her apartment hit him all at once. Stale crackers and dust. Old bacon, rubber boots, petrichor. Mold, rust, and blood. He considers the blood for a moment—he has a feeling about it, an attachment. He follows that feeling into the kitchen, where he can focus on nothing else, though there are plenty of other things to see. He follows it to the kitchen trash can, which he opens, and removes a square of gauze stained brown with blood.

He stares at it. It's his blood, from the gauze that covered the pulled fingernail.

"Did you wake up a vampire?" Niko's voice asks.

"No, he's just discovering his new nose," Ala replies. "Give him a moment."

Dymitr drops the gauze back into the trash. Niko is leaning against the sink, his arms folded, the light of the sun glowing behind his head. The menace that Dymitr used to see in his face isn't gone, exactly. It's just that it no longer creeps up Dymitr's spine the way it used to. Instead, he can see that Niko is beautiful, like a statue of a Roman soldier, like a Kupala Night fire, like a well-made sword.

Niko asks Ala, "Do we call him a 'zmora,' since he's male? Or is he a 'zmoron'?"

Ala laughs. "Technically, it's 'zmór,'" she says. "Though if you want to call him a zmoron, I suppose you can."

Niko smells like powdered sugar, and—Dymitr steps closer, and closer, following his nose to the curve of Niko's neck in a way that would have been embarrassing, if he'd been in his right mind. He touches his nose to Niko's throat, and breathes in. He smells like some kind of flower, and ever-so-slightly of dark chocolate—

"You *are* worried about me," Dymitr says, pulling away. "And . . . a little bit afraid of me?"

Niko's eyes are wide. They skip all over Dymitr's face, and Dymitr wonders how he looks to Niko, if he's still beautiful enough to fight for.

"The word you're looking for," Niko says, "is awe. I am a little in awe of you."

Dymitr opens his mouth to argue, and Niko holds up a hand to stop him.

"Don't," he says. "You'll ruin it."

He curls his fingers under Dymitr's chin and draws him closer. His breath smells like coffee and mint toothpaste. He kisses Dymitr, gentle and slow. It lights up parts of Dymitr he wasn't sure existed, as if the fire that flickers in Niko's eyes has kindled in Dymitr, too.

"See?" Niko says. "It's good to be something new."

The leszy sits on a stump in the Montrose Point Bird Sanctuary, and breathes in the moonlight. A moth flutters around one of his horns, and then settles at the edge of his eye socket, where all the flowers that once grew are now dead, dormant for winter.

He can smell snow in the air, though it hasn't fallen yet. He is as eager for the forest to fall asleep as he will be for it to wake again, come springtime. He enjoys the sound of the trees settling in for their long sleep, and the earth going quiet as all the things that wriggle and scuttle and busy themselves inside it go still. He stretches out one hoof, and listens.

He hears the pressure of footsteps, too light to be human footsteps, and lifts his stag head to see a man standing in the clearing across from him. He carries a bow and quiver. The leszy recognizes him, though it's been months since he last laid eyes on the man's face. He thinks he could even remember the man's name, if he reached for it, but he doesn't. The leszy has never understood the wraith's fixation on names. A leszy has no name, he has only the forest of which he is a guardian.

"He has found me again," the leszy says.

The man nods, and walks closer. The leszy can tell by his movements that he is different than he used to be. No longer human, perhaps. It's a strange thing to observe, since it happens rarely, but it does happen, every now and then. And so he accepts it, as he accepts the changing of the land, the changing of all things.

"I am leaving soon on an errand from Baba Jaga," the man says. "But before I go, I came to test your bow again, if you're willing."

The leszy tilts his head.

"The fern flower won't bloom for several months," he says. "And he will no longer be able to pick it, even so."

"This is just a friendly contest, my lord leszy," the man says. "I no longer have need of the fern flower."

The leszy considers this for a moment.

"Oh," he says at last. "Then let me make a target."

ACKNOWLEDGMENTS

My mother and her three siblings came to this country as children and built a good home for the next generation here. I'm grateful to my grandparents for making that journey with four children in tow, and to my aunts, uncles, and cousins for suffusing my childhood with love, honesty, and good humor, even though our contingent lived across the country from the rest. Special thanks to my uncle Stan for helping me with my Polish and being so encouraging about this story, and to my mother for singing "Gdy się Chrystus rodzi" to me when I was young. I can hear her voice when I read the words.

Thank you:

My editor, Lindsey Hall, for being so enthusiastic about all my ideas, the weird ones and the less-weird ones alike. Her notes made this novella a lot stronger (and bloodier). Joanna Volpe, my agent, who continues to be a rock-solid advocate and friend. Jordan Hill, trusted support, without whom I surely would have lost my mind.

Kristin Dwyer and Sarah Reidy for their publicity expertise and strategic minds; and a special shout-out to Kristin for excellent gifs and that one drive we took without car keys across southern Illinois.

I work with a truly wonderful team at Tor, and I'm

so grateful for them all. For getting my book Out There in every way: Rachel Taylor, Emily Mlynek, Eileen Lawrence, Stephanie Sirabian, Megan Barnard, Andrew Beasley, Becky Yeager, and Yvonne Ye. For getting my books in fine shape to read: Dakota Griffin, Rafal Gibek, Jim Kapp. For making it absolutely drop-dead gorgeous: Heather Saunders, Katie Klimowicz, and Eleonor Piteira (who doesn't work at Tor, but whose art graces this cover). For turning *Crows* into a wonderful audiobook: Elishia Merricks, Claire Beyette, Isabella Navarez, Chrissy Farell, Tim Campbell, James Fouhey, and Helen Laser. For keeping the entire machine running smoothly: Lucille Rettino, Will Hinton, Claire Eddy, Michelle Foytek, Alex Cameron, Rebecca Naimon, Erin Robinson, and Lizzy Hosty. Aislyn Fredsall, for keeping all my many ducks in a row. And of course, Devi Pillai, my publisher, who does not fear the nerds, but loves them (and is them).

New Leaf Literary does great work for my books and books in general, and I am especially grateful to Lindsay Howard, Tracy Williams, Keifer Ludwig, Sarah Gerton, Hilary Pecheone, Eileen Lalley, Kim Rogers, Joe Volpe, Donna Yee, and Gabby Benjamin for that work. Also Pouya Shahbazian and Katherine Curtis, for continuing to find homes for my various projects in the film world, and Goddezz Figueroa for being a pleasure to schedule with. ☺

Adele Gregory-Yao, for keeping me organized (insofar as such a thing is possible) and engaged with the stuff that isn't writing. Bless you, as I often say in the gchat.

A few readers gave me special help as I reached outside

my comfort zone for this book, including Dill Werner, Ennis Bashe, Rafal Gibek (yes, again!), and Magdalena Beata Chuchro. Thank you so much for the thoughtful feedback you offered during the writing process.

Courtney, S, Maurene, Sarah, Zan, Laurie, Kaitlin, Amy, Kate, Michelle, Kara, Margie, Diya, Jen, Morgan, and all the other writers in my life who make this job feel less lonely. All the authors who read this book early and offered supportive quotes, who are wonderful. My friends who aren't writers, who patiently let me explain this completely bananas industry to them on the regular. My family—Rydzes (and Rydz-adjacents), Roths, Rockoviches, Rosses, and Fitches (and Fitch-adjacents)—who support me always.

Years ago, I got to go to Poland to meet readers there, and their excitement to learn that I shared a common ancestry with them is what made me feel okay with exploring it, even though I'm a generation removed. I took some creative license, of course, but know that I'm glad to share these delightful monsters with you. Dziękuję.

Am I gonna thank *The Witcher 3* for getting me excited about Slavic folklore in a new way? Yeah, I guess I am!